THE GHOST OF THE BRIDGE.

A true story based on came across a face-to-face ghost….

I was working as an English tutor to school students at the time duration when I was approached about this terrible incident. According to the prevailing competitive condition in the tuition field of this country, we had to build up a prestigious personal position by improving our personality to be continued the profitable tuition institute in which we were involved in this country. Therefore, competitive advertising campaigns had been periodically launched by us. The staff of the institution gathered at a conference and discussed how to manage the campaign. The principal proposed how to settle the budget for this campaign.

On a relevant day, we had planned to do a poster campaign. Then the tutors had to prepare the posters in relative subjects. The poster artwork and printings should have been completed by the tutors individually. Usually, the printed advertising posters which included the tutors' names and their previous goals should have been displayed on them. The mentioned posters should seemingly be stuck on public notice boards or suitable selected places such as walls, trees or available abandoned buildings to be achieved the expected result. Typically, the tutors had to effectively dedicate the time to be maximized the results of students more than the teachers of the government schools. Unless the tutors wouldn't be able to exist in the field with a successful income. Otherwise, the tutors had gained prestige more than them. We frequently aimed the school students as our victims due to the governmental educational stream of our country collapsed of the teachers' shortcomings, the students' recklessness, especially teaching in the English language and mathematics, and also the lack of governmental provisions for the subjects. Although the appropriate comparative actions should be previously taken to improve English knowledge among the students as it is considered the international language. The government doesn't make an adequate implementation. In a country still being developed, with a poor and weak economy, many young people were idling without being engaged in the proper career opportunities. Therefore, if they had been involved in proper vocational training by improving their English speaking and writing ability, they would be able to appoint to a suitable position at least in a foreign rich country at a significant salary. I wanted to achieve that purpose with my students because I had predictive knowledge as well as my personal philosophy on what is already going on in the country due to the existing corrupted political conduct. I tried to persuade the students they should have gained professional qualifications including fluent English. But I have never told them to ignore other languages.

We had decided to launch the campaign in the nighttime, as it is the most suitable time to launch such a poster campaign. On the mentioned day, we gathered at the institute as we had previously planned. We left our institute to achieve our purpose at about 07.00 pm with our apparatus. The buckets of glue are made by mixing hot water and wheat flour, a coir brush to be applied on the walls, and an adequate bundle of posters. There were four motorcycles with us including a rider, often the subject tutor, and pillion passengers. Then, anyway often the pillion passenger was an adolescent or a previous student of our institute. All of the members were not traveling together as we had to save time. We shared the early prepared posters equally. I had taken four bundles of posters of the other tutors including my ones. I got my helper "Prishan", who was an adolescent student of the institute to the pillion and started the mission to be covered in the earlier selected area. We had planned to cover area by area and expected to be gathered in the same appointed place having completed the first round.

Having concluded nearly half of our workload within about two hours, we all gathered in a night tea cafeteria according to the scheduled plan. A bike in our group was delayed and missed. We took a call for them. They replied to us by the time, at that moment they were on the way. After a few minutes, they came to us. They had been questioned by the night traffic police, as the officials were needed to investigate what kind of posters were with the motorcycle. The police officials in our country are corrupted most of the time. They are conducted as ravenous beasts for bribes from innocent poor people. They had striven to take some money from the above-mentioned motorcyclist. But the tutor who had ridden the motorcycle was an educated, argumentative, intelligent one as he was a university graduate. He knew about the jurisprudence of the country more than that of police officials. However, we had a little rest with some snacks. After having the rest, we started the scheduled duty again to recover the rest of the areas as per our scheduled plan. At about 12.30 pm, we were able to complete the scheduled workload. We returned to the institute and dropped the rest of the things at our institute. So, we enjoyed a few cans of beer with a bottle of alcohol, as a little symposium that had been prepared by the principal of our institute. That was a traditional manner in the field because of we could rarely gather with the staff to be enjoyed. There was only a one third of the bottle has remained. Then the remains quantity offered me by the principal because I was the longest dweller from the institute to be kept with my bag. We discussed the productivity of our mission there at the end and we were paid the previous monthly salaries at the moment. My salary was a considerable amount at the time. Then we scattered.

I had to drop 'Prishan' at his home as he didn't have a way to travel. When we reached his home, the time was about 1.30 am. I never had previously gone to his home. It is situated rather far from the main road about three km. The road wasn't as easy as I thought. His mother opened the door and he entered the home. That lady advised me, "Sir, on which way will you have to go now? Don't ride through the wilderness way, please go along the main road, because you shouldn't ride the bike such the deserted ways at this night". "Okay..., madam, thank you..., good night", I said. She closed the door by telling me "Goodbye and take care". I left them soon without being wasted the time as I was tired, tedious and feeling sleepy. By riding on the shorter way, if omitting the main road, I would be able to reduce by about 23 km. The shortcut was unpopulated and deserted with shanties, shrubs, paddy fields, graveyards and swamps with a long arena. That was the shortest way I had to select as it could be saved my time and fuel wastage due to the unbearable fuel prices in this country. Fossil fuels were very expensive in the country because they had surrendered to unbearable heavy taxes by the government as they were being settled their many wasteful expenses on these taxes. Otherwise, if I would select the shortcut, I will be able to retain my time for about one hour. Then I stopped at the divisional junction. I had to take a strong decision. Normally, I didn't have any hesitation to face a risky challenge. I often have severe morals and self-confidence to be accepted the easiest way, any kind of disturbance whatever will be approached as the repercussions as I have had three glasses of beer. Then I could repel my hesitation. I thought about the tires of the bike are in very good condition. Therefore, if I select the shortcut, I will have been able to escape from the police, as riding with intoxication caused me to be sentenced to a large monetary fund and a suspension of my riding license for six months. Unless, if I will be caught by the police while riding, I will have to pay a considerable amount to the officials as a bribe without filing a lawsuit. I thought for a while, if I would miss this challenge, I won't be a really brave human. I felt a shyness about myself being discouraged my easy way on my cowardliness. I felt a fearsome emotion, even though I had to make a decision as usual in my routine, I don't like to be a coward man. Then I harshly determined. I took out the bottle which remains of alcohol and took a shot and lit a cigarette. I felt an additional power. Yes! If it will have happened anything, no matter I selected the risky and dangerous shortcut. I felt just isolated emotion. But I had already built my mind. I had a fully charged powerful torch, a cigarette lighter, a pack of cigarettes with a few, and some essential stuff in my backpack which was hanging out my back.

I turned to the deserted and arduous road. Of course, the road wasn't a bed of roses but also with muddy pits, covered with huge trees. But the track was not so hard and it was not as difficult as I thought earlier because the vehicles and motorcycles had been traveled only in the daytime. There was an advantage, it had not rained in the last few days. I could see the track clearly because of my powerful headlight. I made sure to balance my proper speed according to the road and especially continue my concentration. I was sure, there weren't wild beasts like lions, tigers, leopards, bears, or elephants in this area because this arena was surrounded by large cities in the country. I usually was familiar with riding such paths, which means narrow roads in the thicket because once or twice I have been

involved in hunting at night time with an old friend called **Kaluwa**. I continually rode the bike and my thoughts aroused a forgone time duration in my past.
While I was working as a clerk in a huge governmental industry in the eastern province of the country, I had so many friends because I didn't select the title of the person or rank of them to be made friendships. Kaluwa also worked as a boiler operator in the distillery of that industry. He used to engage in hunting on his holidays as a pastime. He invited me to gather with them for hunting. I had a huge desire to see their hunting. But, before entering the journey, I said that I will never participate to help killing or even touching the killed animals. I wanted only to have an experience of hunting. I have never used a gun or will never use it. Then we planned to involve hunting on a full moon night. I took stuff with a powerful torch, fully safely dressed in boots and a cap. They gave me a bag with some stuff including a nylon rope ladder. But it was not with considerable heavy. Kaluwa and his assistant also dressed properly. The loaded double-barrel shotgun was with Kaluwa. The regular assistant of Kaluwa was equipped with a hunting knife and gave me another knife for my protection. We had to row in a lake to be entered the jungle.

Kaluwa and the assistant advised me to take a cudgel with me to lead it when traveling in the jungle because there would be early tied guns by the poachers in the daytime. If there will be such tied guns, definitely there will be a thread that is adapted to the trigger of the gun. The dreadful crocodiles were there in this lake because I had seen them in the daytime while I was riding my bike on the embankment of that lake. I thought, whether attacked them in our small row, what can we do? However, after rowing for about half an hour, we landed on the lake bank. The assistant tied the row with a tree and got the stuff. Now we are in the jungle. Kaluwa had expected to hunt a wild boar, a deer, an elk, or any kind of adequate animal. While rowing, he advised me on how to behave in the jungle. Sometimes, there may be elephants, snakes, or tigers on the way. He taught me we should have escaped them. Hunting in such a dangerous jungle is not as easy as I early thought. I felt severe dreadful thoughts about why I gathered with them. Although, now I can't return! Before entering the jungle, Kaluwa took a bottle of alcohol made from the distillery of our industry. We called them, spirits. However, it was a stolen bottle from the distillery. We had some small glasses of liquor. Of course, not for the intoxication, and only for missing the fear. We had a precious service of a brightly shining moon at this moment. I suffered the beauty of the lake and I saw the opposite side of the embankment where we rode on some daytimes. I had never experienced such a beautiful attraction of lake. The time was really 11.35 pm. We had a taste of the cigarettes and started hunting. Kaluwa led with the gun, the assistant followed him, and I chased them. There was a footpath laid into the jungle because it was the usual way used by the hunters and poaching people. We slowly, observantly, and inaudibly entered the deep and thicker jungle. We were unable to find a suitable animal apart from a small rabbit and a small hedgehog. Kaluwa usually doesn't hunt small animals. We walked further. Suddenly, Kaluwa stopped and inaudibly said, "There may be an elephant nearby this area. Then we mustn't waste our time, let's go back to the tree hut soon!". "What is the tree hut?" I wanted to ask, but it wasn't a suitable time. I had to follow them. We reached an open grassy area only with three huge trees. There was a huge stone and two well-grown trees. A nice tree hut had been made on a tree.

"Let's climb up soon, take the rope ladder, and hurry up men!" Kaluwa said. I took the ladder out of my back sack and gave it to the assistant. The assistant aimed the torch light on the tree hut and checked carefully. Kaluwa said, "The elephants are coming here soon, hurry up!" How he guesses about a herd of elephants was there and coming our way? The assistant climbed up the tree and throw down the nylon rope ladder. I climbed up with my stuff, rather a difficult job. I was able to climb up soon and Kaluwa followed with the gun. "Waw! It is a very nice view, a miraculous attraction!" I said. I have to solve some questions. I impatiently waited a moment and asked, "How would you suspect early, there will be an elephant nearby?" Kaluwa said, "There were a few dungs of elephant and the nocturnal birds had hastily flown away from their perches. Otherwise, I heard a fine sound of breaking branches and the hissing of an elephant!". "We didn't hear such a sound, isn't it", I asked the assistant. He said, "The regular hunters have the scent of animals. They meticulously listen to the jungle and have practiced the instinct of a sleuth". Kaluwa advised us to be silent and listen to the surroundings. We didn't speak apart from muttering.

Within about four minutes, a few elephants entered, actually a very nice herd of elephants very slowly came out of the thicket. They passed that open area and gradually passed the tree hut toward the lakeside. We didn't make any kind of noise at the moment. They sometimes stopped, aroused the dust, shook their ears, and hoisted their trunks. They freely shifted on their way. Suddenly one of them started to trumpet. The moon fabulously helped us to be seen them very nicely.

I thought, how lucky person I was to be seen as such a fantastic and picturesque seen on a brightly shining moon. "They would come back within a few hours on this way because they went to the lakeside to drink water. When they passed, we took a little small shot of liquor and smokes. I suffered the surroundings that I could see the huge overview from the tree hut. I stealthily wished to miss hunting any kind of animal on this night. If they early had known about my expectation, I will never have had this chance to walk and watch such fantastic events. I asked how and who built this super tree hut in this place. Kaluwa said, "There was a Ganja plantation through the vegetables in this place long ago. When it was growing, the planters had to protect themselves from the police and the animals. They had built this hut durably roofing with asbestos sheets. The floor had been made with energetic planks. Because they needed to take overviews of the area. Some police officers had been knowing about this place and they had enjoyed being here with the owner of the place. The owner had prodigally wasted and treated the police officers. Then the place is protected and the owner also had become a millionaire. Otherwise, the owner of the cannabis plantation was a famous indigenous physician in the country and he used that crop for his medicinal productions. There had been a nice iron ladder to be climbed up and down with leaning the tree, but it had been stolen by someone a few months ago.

Then we got down from the tree hut. We had to walk for about two hours in the jungle and finally, Kaluwa was able to hunt a big wild boar. They converted it to pork. I didn't involve in any kind of help for that workload. We were able to reach our homes at about six a.m. Kaluwa had sent some kilos of pork to me.

By thinking about the previous memorials, I continually rode for half an hour along the road. While I was riding, there was a grave yard. It had expanded both sides of the road. I have heard early, if the inhuman souls and ghosts were in the graveyard, we should loudly shout with obscene words as well as we know. But I have never believed on that expression, but I should reveal the truth based on my heart, I also have a severe hesitation to pass such a graveyard even in the day time if not being taken with a drink. However, that expression is true or false, I started to tell bad words, but also I was able to find only three such the lascivious words at the moment.

Then I loudly shouted, “I will never scare you, f...ing ghosts, if you can, foolish f...ers come and attack me, bastard and illegitimate dogs” There wasn’t any kind of such a trouble with me. But I encouraged to increase my speed at the graveyard.
The time was about a quarter to two, no one restricted me this night, no obstacles on my way, no external and disruptive headlights from the vehicles, only the headlight of my own. No feelings about the cold as I had worn a nice waterproof jacket, and trousers with shoes to be covered my whole body with the visor helmet. I carefully rode on my way, but I cared to detain my concentration as well as I could, because wild animals may cross the road such as boars, rabbits, foxes, polecats, or even wild dogs. I suddenly saw a very big tree had laid across the road while I was taking a bend. “Oh! What is this?” I arduously stopped the bike. The road is completely blocked. I got a fear about me because this huge log can be kept by thieves or robbers to be robbed me. I hurriedly remembered my purse with my salary. But I aimed my headlight to realize this urgent roadblock, but it was a large python. I suddenly get back the bike away from it about five meters. Because I was a little delay to stop the bike according to my speed. I didn’t turn off my engine because the headlight should have been aimed at the huge python. It is being slowly crossed the road. I had to stay about ten minutes to its moving. I approached a quick fear, if this mad snake was with hunger, couldn’t it suddenly turn and catch me. Then I raised my accelerator. Despite not having any external ears, snakes can actually hear quite a range of low sounds. They can hear sounds in the 80-600 Hz range, and since the human voice ranges from 85—255 Hz, then snakes can indeed hear this this bike raising sound.

Having its crossed, I restarted riding for about 35 minutes and I was able to reach a plain and open area. Typically, at the night, however, such as midnight this time there were no more clouds in the sky, were blinking stars far away, I saw the full moon shining brightly in the sky and the fluttering paddy fields and banana trees on the breeze. I wanted to stop my riding to be seen the beauty of the environment in the moonlight because I prefer to enjoy these beautiful surroundings. Certainly, I stopped on a little narrow bridge where easier to have a better view as I wanted to suffer the landscape and take a rest with a cigarette. The severe necessity of smoking felt me a little bother because of my beer-alcoholic background. However, I cared to keep an adequate space with the edge of the bridge, because there weren't security fences which means bridge arms beside the bridge. The depth might be about over 8 feet with the stream because the eddy currents have emerged. The flowing stream seemed to be floating with the blinking stars because of the reflection of moonbeams.

I took off my helmet and relaxed the jacket, leaning on the bike. I wanted to refill with another shot from the bottle and lit a cigarette. While tasting it, watched all around the attractive surroundings. A monitor, a large tropical lizard with a long neck, and a narrow head were there on the stream bank. I took my torch and watched it to have a better view as I knew early, the monitors were formerly believed to give early warning of crocodiles. Fortunately, it was not a greedy crocodile. According to the place where I stopped, even also a dangerous and ravenous crocodile might be there in the water.

But it was an isolated, fantastic and miraculous environment. Breaking down the tranquility, I heard a sharp ululating of an animal but had no idea whether a dog or a fox. I felt rather smell of mud. Heard a sound of an owl with various yells and with scary, ferociously hooting noises of the nocturnal creatures. A slightly strong wind was blown with a severe cold. I sucked the final pull of the cigarette and threw down the butt onto the flowing water. It disappeared soon with a vortex. Having enjoyed the appreciation of the view, just rang my mobile phone. Oh! My wife had been waiting for me without having her dinner. "Get sleep, I am still on the way, don't bother about me, I will be there at home within one and a half hours", I replied to her. I restarted the journey. After a few minutes, suddenly, I saw a person coming towards me beyond about forty meters along the plain way, I supposed he or she was a person who traveled any kind of own urgent necessity.

I didn't take that person into my account. By considering it an ordinary event, I continued my way. I extremely wanted to ignore him. Suddenly the person rushing reached out to stop me by waving his hand. I couldn't choose a quick decision whether should I stop or not. But I felt there is a person who is in a trouble and trying to get help. Quickly I stopped my motorcycle. But I didn't stop the engine. I intended to leave him soon. My headlight also was on. I extremely wanted to miss him as soon as possible. This unanticipated encounter completely distracted my mind! What kind of a man may here be at this owlish time on the way? The man who was there with wearing a headscarf in front of me. Yes! Now he is in front of me. I couldn't link my voice as it has shaken my soul. I took a deep breath into my heart. A very thinner heat with a hard twinge was aroused quickly in my stomach and it was scattered along my head. The ears warmed up. The beating of my heart increased rapidly. The blood circulation rose. In short, a horrible experience. I felt a severe cold at once. I had adhered frequently, that deep inhalation is the most effective result and the most suitable remedy for such tragical events. Yes! I immediately experimented with it. Now, I reformed into a prudent condition. I was able to recover my presence.

I asked loudly, "yes! Tell me! What is the trouble with you, have you been disoriented or don't you have any shelter?" Without being told anything, the headscarf that had been worn by the person was slowly removed by himself. I couldn't believe my own eyes. Ahhh! A miraculous moment. There was a beautiful, enchanting girl. Actually, a young, innocent girl! Her delightful eyes fluttered. Her face shone brightly in my headlight. A sexy young girl aged among 20 to 30. She tried to smile. Suddenly I remembered a famous film actress that I have seen previously. I became a very hard confuse because of her beauty. Her forehead was as like as a crescent, her lips were as like as immature buds, her breasts were as like as the couple of swans, her hip was as like a beautiful and circular bed of roses. Her thighs were as like as the mostly persuasive to kissing them.

Her wavy hair fluttered in the breeze and bothered her. She tried to control it. Her soft reddish blouse and light bluish skirt fluttered by annoying her. She didn't try to control it. Her very thinner light bluish blouse had torn or opened from the front side, I could see clearly her nude round breasts through the lacy bra and round, filled thighs as the skirt also let her roam freely with the breeze. I suddenly felt an unavoidable and marvelous lust. Her thinner and invisible under skirt didn't try to prevent the violence of the breeze through her inviting and enchanting thighs.
"What do you want, is there any trouble with you?" I asked again.
She replied, "Would you take me to the nearest town please?" Her voice was very gentle and had an alluring beauty. It was just like a prior inducement to be made me ride with her. No more time to waste, I should have taken a decision soon. Yes! I had the most suitable decision.
I was exactly confused. This is impossible. This may be a planned trap. The relatives of this girl might ambush me among nearby bushes, to be robbed me, and plunder my bicycle according to the prevailing position in this country. Even if they killed and hide my body after the robbery, they'll be unable to find anything. My dead body will be hidden by the swamp which laid through the mangrove forest for a few days. My dead body will never be allowed to expose this felony, as the ravenous appetite of huge monitors and crocodiles. I will be forever disappeared from my innocent wife, young beautiful, and innocent daughter, and my young brave handsome son. The altered motorcycle will have been sold and it will be running on the way without my fuel. The salary that I earned during the last month will be lavishly spent by this fabulous girl and her companions. I linked my words hard, "If you don't want me to cheat or mislead, I would like to help you!" She said, "I want to be taken my emancipation, I think you will help me." Then I replied, "I would like to help you, but now is not for a suitable time!"

My wife...will never believe this exodus. What will have happened to the reputation which I had earned during my lifetime as a tutor in this area? If I would prefer to give a lift for her. No! I should escape from this suddenly encountered unanticipated woman. As a prestigious teacher, as a respectable father, as an exemplary husband, extremely I must leave her. The beautiful girl who stimulated erotic feelings was left open and didn't try to rearrange the top buttons of her blouse and smiled slightly. One of her yellowish ivory naked breasts could be seen through the previous lacework bra as not much covered them. Her cleavage also was considerably open, and I could slightly see her tan nipple points through the thin lacy bra. I felt I should have taken her on to the pillion. Her murmurs voice again, "Can you keep me alone in this arduous arena?" There wasn't a distance between us more than one meter. I could see her barefoot slightly. She had come to the road without slippers. A complicated doubt! How she walked without her slippers on this rough floor? I didn't have any other option unless speaking with her.

"Okay! I said, can you ride my bicycle with me?" I wanted to reduce my risk. Because, while riding the bicycle, she is unable to make me a dangerous event as I am on her back. Unless when I allow her to sit as my pillion, she will be able to lead me to her purpose, or she will be able to squeeze my neck or get me in trouble with any kind of knife. "Oh! No, I am not familiar with riding, otherwise, as I early expected, you can't identify me, and that means you are not the person I am expecting. But I can send a message with you to the community about me, that is the reason why I selected you at this moment", she said. What was the meaning of her last expression? Another complicated doubt. I suddenly realized; she is expecting someone. That means, her expectation would already may be coming on the way. Then I instantly decided to leave her.

"I am so sorry. I will try to catch a taxi for you and send you to the next town", I said while raising the accelerator. Then she loudly said, "Whenever you will have to help me!" "Okay, I will send a taxi for you soon, If I will be unable to find a taxi, I promise you, I'll be back soon, then please wait." I said and leave the clutch. Suddenly, I left her alone on the way. I rode the bicycle on my way as quickly as I could. I didn't have any idea about her, or what kind of a young woman was she. Why did she go there, near that unbelievable time, and without a caretaker? Finally, I decided that she might be a member of an organized robbers' gang. I rode the bike on my way, but my mind restricted my journey because I felt like I have missed a person's liability when one's burden. I couldn't be left her in such a dangerous event if actually she was in a trouble. Otherwise, why should I be scared to a woman! Then, I decided to help her. I took a harsh decision to be returned. I stopped the bike and turned back without thought twice. While I was riding back, I observed beside the way for about three minutes whether would there be any risky events or not, I could reach the bridge which I stopped early. But also, I couldn't find anything, even any evidence about the girl. I made the headlight around the bridge and the way and the place where I met her. There wasn't any sign of the relevant girl. I wanted to clear my doubt about whether she was there or not. I felt a little fear, then left the idea of finding her. I started to remove the place soon. While riding for about 15 minutes, I approached the main road. There was a taxi stopped beside the way, I expected to describe the event of the girl whom I was talking to near the bridge, with the driver of the taxi. I stopped my bike in front of him, but he was highly sleeping on the adapted driving seat as a bed, then I gave up the idea. I didn't waste my time to further inquire about her. I selected my way to reaching my home. However, while I was riding, I thought, I shouldn't have missed her, I nicely had to make a fantastic and memorable night with her, if I had built an enthusiasm to involve her to giving a lift. I had to inquisitive about her further, because of her beautiful figure. If I was as an unmarried person, I would be enjoyed with her. But I should have more thoughtful about my children, my wife and my prestige and about my students.

There was a regular police roadblock, which meant a barrier for searching the nocturnal vehicles, whether illegal transportation or driving intoxicated. Fortunately, I early knew about this barrier, then I got off the bike and started to push it because if I will be caught having liquor, there will be a court case because the beer and alcoholic smell definitely would be identified by them. Then, an officer asked, "Why are you pushing the bike, is there any problem with you?" I decided to tell him the truth. I said, "I have taken a little can of beer, then I rode the bike until I was reaching near the checkpoint and I intended that after I will pass this barrier, I will be supposed to start riding again because I should have made respected the officials of the police department and the existing law". Then he asked, "Where did you go at this night?" I explained to him that we had done early and the reason for my delay. Then he appreciated me about my honesty and released me after having my details. Further he told me, "Don't try to ride fast, you will have to be faced in any trouble." I thanked him and pushed the bike until passing the checkpoint.

I was able to reach my home within about one hour of time duration, after leaving that girl without helping on the road. I suffered from severe repentance, whether she wanted a really help from me? The reason why I neglected the protection of that girl who was disoriented in a dreadful place amidst a forest.

In the morning I described the event with my wife that I was faced with last night. She just kidding, "You should have carried her into the home". But I know, if I had given her a lift and committed a dreadful condition, my wife will never be forgiven me. The next time, I got a phone call, from the principal of the institute, Mr. **Dinuja Disanayaka**. Extremely I wanted to inform the incident that I faced last night. Usually, I had an amicable friendship with him. We spoke about all kinds of private matters whatever were with personal or official positions between us. He was an unmarried person. He worked very friendly with us. He was a civil engineer and maintained a tuition institute as a part-time earning engagement. I saw him as a good manager, and a good organizer, and I was able to study him as an energetic and talented person with hard determination. He always didn't punish the students, but also, punished or dismissed the impaired students who committed drugs. I had worked with more principals such as the tuition institutes. Many conductors were used to instruct the teaching even if they couldn't highly understand the subject. But also, Dinuja had never poked the subject if the teacher had done his duty according to the syllabus. Once I have involved in another institution. The principal of that always changed his principles and bothered the teachers to reload the unnecessary workload. He always criticized the teachers and never appreciate anyone even though we have done our work to increase the knowledge of the students. But Dinuja was an ideal person for a principal. He managed everything very excellent disciplinary manner. He had a beautiful, enchanting, and talkative innocent girlfriend who was opposed by his parents. He took my instructions on how to win his parents' willingness for that girl. I taught him, how to balance the parents' party without engaging in any confusion. Then I taught him to let time impatiently. Otherwise, he also was a mathematics teacher in the institute. I described the entire incident with him.

He told me, "If I were you, I would never leave her, and if she was such a beautiful girl as you said, I will take her in to a hotel room". He laughed, loudly, and said further, "She might be a ghost, don't you believe the apparitions?" I told him, "No I have never believed the inhuman souls". "That is the reason you didn't frighten that woman, if you had felt a fearful mentality at the time, you would have confused, in your confusion, she may ascend your body and lead you to a nearest graveyard." he said. However, he promised to further inquire about the girl who appeared near the bridge. He called back me after a while. He had taken a phone call to Prishan and then he had told him, that he doesn't know about a haunt or anything about being appeared a ghost that way. But Dinuja had emerged on a doubtful mind on Prishan's replying. Because Prishan's sound had differed at the moment. The time had flown stealthily without being told by anyone. Usually, our duties are regularly done by us.
According to my timetable in that institution, I had to involve three days per week in teaching the students. I had involved with also other few institutions, therefore, I was busy. We, the staff regularly gathered at the interval and spoke about the incident that I approached. Then we have taken the conclusion that the girl who appeared to me that night at the bridge might be a ghost. I decided to pay attention to the ghosts and inhuman souls. I gathered more information about them.

The inhuman spirit is an occasion of human fundamental theories of mind faculty and psychology, with the spiritual or mental part of the dead person or in an animal's mind. While the term can be used with the same meaning as "inhuman soul". The inhuman spirit is a powerful wave, sometimes used to refer to the impersonal, universal, or considerable stage of human or animal nature in contrast to a soul which can refer to a mental image of a person or animal that died, and after his or its death, is expecting for reincarnation. The human spirit includes our intellect, emotions, fears, passions, and creativity with a bodily appearance. But the inhuman soul can be defined as a dead person's mind wave which is mighty floating or existing in the space between the time duration of rebirth as a wave. The waves cannot be destructed but also can be changed. Because it has consisted of considerable power.

The human spirit is considered to be mentally empowered with naturally born and naturally grown by a mother on the world functions with understanding, thinking, feelings, judgments, passion, lust, imaginative power, and intelligence. Humans can be distinguished from the separate component of the mind which comprises the entities of emotion, images, memory, and activities, and with each contrasting personality.

The human spirit consists of love, intelligence, and creative action and with a social construct representing the qualities of attentive purpose and meaning which transcend each individual human.

A ghost can be defined as the soul or spirit of a dead person or animal that can be appeared to already living people. The ghosts are widely formed from invisible influential psychological waves, see-through or scarcely visible straggly shapes, to realistic or lifelike forms. The inhuman souls are called a few different words by the people such as apparition, haunt, phantom, poltergeist, shade, specter, spook, wraith demon, or ghost.

There is a traditional belief in our community, in the existed people in the past believed in an afterlife, as the expressions of the spirits of the dead, are widespread, dating back to animism which means the belief in a supernatural power that organizes the material universe or worshiping in pre-literate cultures. In some religious cults of funeral rituals, exorcisms, and some practices of spiritualism are specifically described to rest the spirits of the dead. Ghosts are typically described as solitary, human-like essences, though stories of ghostly armies and the ghosts of animals rather than humans have also been recounted. They are believed to haunting in the familiar locations, objects, or people whom they were associated with in life. Despite more amount of investigation, there is no scientific evidence that any location is inhabited by the spirits of the dead persons. Because the existing scientists still unable to reveal what is the mind, where is located the mind of the body and where is the destination of its power.

However, that incident was forgotten and we further didn't follow of it.

During my adolescent period, I was preferred to be an actor and involve in the artistic creations. I had gained an ability to acting on the stage dramas and performed few events. When I was involved in a career as a general clerk in a reputed industry and later promoted as purchasing officer, I created a stage drama while I was working because I was selected as the Recreational Secretary of the industry. The rural young people were selected for the characters. There were genius young girls and boys in my drama as the performing stars. A boy was there called "**Palitha Iddagoda**", was very talented for all, including sports, music, singing and playing instruments. Later after his university studies, he was selected to the police department as an S.I, that means sub inspector. During that period, I had to leave from my existed job that I have ever engaging with severe satisfaction, because of the weakened, short-sighted administrative management by the former government of the country. That industry was polluted by the politicalized union leaders. Then I had to leave from the region and came to the capital city to be found a suitable profession. I found a few jobs, and involved for a few years. I had an ability to teaching. Then I committed to the tuition field. I was able to gain a successful income without being bothered. One day, I received a phone call from that boy, **Palitha Iddagoda** had promoted as an I.P of the police department. He had received a transfer from his rural station to capital city. Then he had taken his first appointment as an I.P, in my tuition area. He came to my home before reporting his duty. Then I also was able to associate with some officials of the police. During this period, I gathered a prestigious place in my field because my students were being taken high marks and high results of my subject. Then I didn't try to involve with the slave-like jobs.

There was a concert of our institution for passing out of the students. We had arranged a party with a musical event, the students were the singers. We had arranged a famous orchestra for the music. I also had to sing an individual song. Then we enjoyed and were able to renew the friendships of the former students. That was rather an excellent and well-arranged party, the staff would have been participated with their family. There had also been invited the old students and the parents of them. Prishan also had participated with his mother, and sung a song beautifully. Then I had an occasion to speak with him and his mother, he had intended to be married recently. I also would be invited for the wedding. Prishan's mother was a very calm and captivating lady. I was introduced to her by Prishan, as I had gone her home at that night to be dropped him.

After a few months, our staff of the institution was invited the wedding ceremony of Prishan. I had to participate for the wedding with my son because my son also familiar with my institution as a student. Then I decided to involve in the ceremony with him. It was held in Prishan's home, because the land and the home were more spacious. The ceremonial time was 10.30 am to 4.30 pm. There was a liquor bar whether the needs of participants availability of liquor with lunch. I have travelled there with my son on my motorcycle because I didn't have a car at the moment as I had sold my car.

We left the home about 9.00 am. I wanted to see the bridge that girl appeared me, to be investigated the surroundings, because I had a harsh necessity to search the place in a daytime. Then I rode the bike with my son on that way. I stopped the bike on the bridge and I described every event with my son, how I met her and from where she appeared on to the road. He also was a bigger curiosity to learn about haunts and ghosts. According to his request, I promised him to be described later in proper time all of the events I had approached early relative with the adventures and dreadful events in my lifetime. However, we spent about 25 minutes on the bridge and relative place that girl appeared me. We were able to involve with the wedding ceremony about 11.00 am. The staff of our institution also had participated. The first ceremonial event of the traditional wedding had been started. It is called Traditional Marriage ceremony.
It is a traditional wedding custom. The ceremony takes priority on a little stage, which is conducted on a beautifully decorated, traditional wooden platform. The ceremonial customs involve as a series of traditional rituals adhered by the bride and groom. The groom and his relatives stand on the right side of the platform and

the bride's family stands at the left side. The bride and groom climb on the stage leading with the right foot first. They worship by genuflecting to the parents and the nearest adults and welcome each other with palms held together in the traditional manner. The early managed ceremony officiant then presents betel leaves to the couple and says stanzas, which they accept them and hand back to him to be dropped them on the little stage.

The bride's father places the right hand of the bride on that of the groom as a symbolic gesture of officially handing over the bride to the groom. Hence, that possess of the bride is traditionally symbolize to bride groom. The groom's brother hands over a tray with seven sheaves of betel leaves with a coin placed in each. The groom holds the tray while the bride takes one leaf at a time and drops it on the little stage. The groom then repeats this process. The groom's brother hands a gold necklace to the groom who in turn places it on the bride's neck. A brother who consanguine with mother's party, that means uncle enters the stage and ties the small fingers of the bride and groom with a golden colored thread and then pours water with a little kettle over the fingers. Six girls will then bless the marriage with The Buddhist stanzas. The groom presents to his bride a white cloth which in turn is presented to the bride's mother. This is an expression of the groom's gratitude and honor to his mother-in-law. The bride's mother should offer a plate of milk rice specially cooked for this custom to the bride who feeds a piece to the groom. The groom then feeds the bride back. As the newly married couple steps down from the stage, the groom's family member should break a fresh coconut dividing to same two parts.

Having being ended the customary events of Prishan's wedding, we enjoyed the treatments as well as our needs. I went to the liquor bar for a few times, but also, I definitely took in to my account, not to be overtake my capacity because I will have to ride on the main road with my son. Otherwise, I have usually practiced to confine around my limit. Unless I will be punished by my wife with a tons of blaming. However, the staff members of our institute had cared to be more decent in the ceremony, because we were the teachers of a famous tuition institute of the area. Our students and their parents are also had participated for the wedding. Then traditionally, the new couple left the home for their honeymoon.

After a few years, as I think about nine or ten years later of above wedding ceremony, I had to participate in the funeral of Prishan's grandmother, because Prishan was a good friend and a genus old student of our institute. The funeral was conducted in their family graveyard and the cremation had arranged in itself. The funeral started at about 3.30 pm. I reached home of Prishan at 2.00 pm and helped the pre-arrangements. Our principal and a few teachers had participated.

After the traditional customs of the funeral with the cremation of the grandmother's coffin, we were gathered in to the front yard of Prishans home. Usually at such the occasions, we used to have some liquor. Our principal had bought two bottles. At the time about 8.30 pm. Then we had more time to speak each other. I wanted to speak about the previous incident when I was approached on the bridge, whether such an event had been happened early or after on that bridge. Because I had decided to go home that time also on the same shortcut.

Prishan also participated with us as he was being worked as an accountant in a reputed company at the moment. Meanwhile, we were speaking, and that incident was described by me to them. There were approximately about seven people, all of our companions.

Prishan's mood changed and he wanted to personally speak with me. I went away with him to a nearby convenience place by missing the friends. Prishan said, "There is a hidden enigma with that event, then we shouldn't speak about that incident in the open crowded space, because there may be the barbers by spying of the participants in this moment". Then I agreed with him and we postponed the discussion for a few minutes till the crowed thinning.

He also already had some liquor and started to speak. "Sir, I still remember that date, you came to be dropped me even if I was about sixteen, my mother advised you to don't go by that shortcut. Do you still remember her advice?" "Yes! Actually, I had to select the easiest way to keep my economical fuel waste", I said.

"There was a full moon in the sky that night. Do you remember, sir?" "Yes, everything I remember, like it had happened right just now", I replied. "Do you really remember her face?" "Yes, she has really appeared as a beauty queen".

Our principal, Mr. Dinuja Disanayaka came to us, and said, "May I come, please? "Okay, Sir, Come and sit here, I will be back soon with something", said Prishan and left us. I told Dinuja about what was our topic.

Prishan came back with five photographs of beautiful girls. "Please tell me whose photo is similar to that girl you had seen on the bridge that day"? I selected one of them without any hesitation and I said, "I'm definitely sure this is the photo." He looked the photo and said, "You are correct, Sir, Now I will tell you the true story about my aunt!" "Aunt???, How she was your aunt?", I astonished. "Yes, she was my mother's own elder sister, who was being studied at the University of the Capital city. She was a beauty queen in that university and a captivating girl who had expected to be a graduate." Then our curiosity was aroused. He started again, "As my mother says, during the school years of my aunt, a young boy who lived in this village had hoped to be made a love congruity with my aunt, "**Nirasha**". But she didn't expect to be involved in a love affair due to her studies. She was the Team captain of the Net-ball game in the university, had an inherited delicate and flexible body shape that had been given by the nature for the girls to be automatically attract and enchant the boys.

The priority was given by her for the studies. She had been additionally played a key role of her school as the leader in the debate team, music band, and the sports side and had given a priority to playing net-ball. That the boy also was in her school student, but also didn't have any prominent genius for the studies, any significant subject or sports event. That boy called **Tiran,** was an only son of the chairman of provincial council in the area. His father was an influential rich man with political powers. Then his son, Tiran had infested to Nirasha for her inclining to love affair. She had been refused his request for a long time. Tiran had written the love letters to Nirasha and he had sent her those with his most reliable friend, **Kiththa.** Although she had refused them and returned without being accepted. One of his love letters had caught to the class teacher of Tiran and had submitted to the principal. Tiran was punished and advised by the principal. Tiran was grieved and gradually approached an anger with Nirasha. Then Tiran had arranged to raid her on the way from school to home of Nirasha. Tiran usually had done it with Kiththa, and **Podde.** Podde was also one of his immoral friends of Tiran who neglected the studies and absconded from the school. Then Nirasha's mother usually had to being engaged to fetch her.

Nirasha involved the studies as well as her best and selected to the university in her first time of the Advanced Level examination. She had studied in the governmental university of capital city in the country. While she was studying in university, there has been arranged an excursion to visit countryside of the country as an assignment of the students researching project. A handsome and prestigious boy who was being studied in her faculty was encouraged on Nirasha. The boy had submitted a love proposal to her, but also, she did hesitate at the first time to give her priority for the boys or love affairs. After a few months, having more details of the boy such as his behavior, personality, qualitative aspects and external figure. She had been approached in an affair with him at that moment. His name was **Pranama Jayasooriya**, was an intelligent and senior student. They behaved very politely as the lovers. Because of Nirasha doesn't involve to any kind of misconducting according to her ethical background. But she had informed to her family about this affair. He had come often to our home and my grandparents had agreed to the said affair because of he was an educated and peaceful person. His parents were government teachers. The boy had grown in a peaceful, well-mannered and obediently in the adults. After this connection, he had built an intimate friendship with our mother's family. According to my memory, I remember that my father had said once recently, that Mr. Pranama Jayasooriya was appointed later as **a lawyer** in the high court in the capital city.

Meanwhile, that boy, Tiran who lived in this village had been requested my aunt's love several times by annoying her. My aunt, Nirasha had continually refused the requests of Tiran. Tiran also had stopped his studies and had been started some businesses such as building constructions and highways constructions with his father's help. His father, that chairman of provincial council had passed some governmental contracts to his son. But he didn't have any knowledge about the subject, had been hired a staff for the workload. Tiran wandered with his playful friends in the restaurants, having with liquor parties.
Prishan continued the story. Some friends of Prishan were going to leave and wanted to farewell from him. He attended for the friends. We decided to know the story with complete events. Our curiosity had aroused to be known everything.
"Let's have a little more, I want to continue". Don't you feel like?" Dinuja asked.
"Yes, shall I bring the bottle and glasses here," I said. Then Prishan returned and said, "No! Please wait I would take them soon", Prishan left. "A fabulous story, it is just like a film story. I never thought that the incident what you said would be a true incident", Dinuja was amazed. After a few minutes, Prishan came back with the necessary stuff. Having been settled with the stuff, Prishan restarted.
"Then, she was 23 years. Nirasha always traveled without parental guidance because only my mother which means Nirasha's sister had alone in the home, as my mother also was a little girl at the time. Nirasha's all expenses had to cover at the punctual time. Therefore, my grandfather had to involve with his businesses. My grandmother was always detained in the home due to she was a housewife. My grandfather was a businessman. He was being considered about my aunt, Nirasha's protection, but not at always because of his busier life on his business. Otherwise, they didn't have seen any threatened social environment at that period of time as Nirasha rarely came to home. Nirasha's parents had thought the threatened condition has been thinned after her university selection and Tiran also had involved with his businesses.
Tiran was a tyrannical and playful boy, and was only non-educated son of a rich family. He had only his father's money how he unjustifiably earned by exploiting the innocent people. His father was a chairman of the provincial council of the province. He had a political mighty in the area. However, as a politician, he dominated the area. He had appointed a few thugs who might be engaged any kind of barbarian work for his protection. Usually, the disgusting politicians of this country are commonly corrupted, immoral and always laundering the government taxes and exploiting the innocent populace despite the inflation of the country was being developed. The sons such as the politicians of the country also were barbarian creatures within their stupid behavior. Since the time of adolescent, the brutal aspects were ascended with them due to the shameless father's shameless and unpleasant consanguinity. After a few months, Tiran had again trended to Nirasha, because his revenging mind didn't allow to stay her freely. He early had openly expressed a few times, Nirasha will never be allowed to marry any other person.
Tiran had been using an imported, expensive motorcycle. When my aunt, Nirasha was going to university and returning at the weekends, Tiran followed her and had threatened her about the neglecting of him. Tiran had built up a huge wave of anger with my aunt and consequently, his love had been converted into hate with

my aunt. Later failing his effort, he infested her. He had wanted to revenge on her. He had promised with his friends, that if she doesn't assent to him, she won't be allowed to marry another person. But my aunt Nirasha didn't have cared for him. She had continually refused his unilateral love. Nirasha was intelligent with well-mannered behavior and she had built a strong concentration and high imaginative power surrounded with the Buddhist Philosophy.

Buddhist philosophy refers to the philosophical investigations and systems of inquiry or quest of how developing the internal waves of a human mind by well-mannered practices of meditation to made the path for liberation. I have read more articles about Buddhism and how to make the deliverance of the soul of a human being. But I never have found a real, simple or clear explanation of meditation that how to meditate, and how to beginning for realistic and proper mind making path to meditation. As my capacity, what is the meditation? The mind waves matching with the blood circulation, heart beat and with respiration can be simply defined as meditation. Practicing the meditation very carefully, the mind imaginative power can be fabulously improved in a person. While meditating, the person should have been practiced to remove every concept of desires from his mind and omission of physical objects. Within a few minutes, after starting the meditation, the mind goes to relax plight by emerging yellowish background and gradually meditative person's mind should have become to a very pure and immaculate position. After he should concentrate his mind to his aim. If someone can practice this regularly, he will be able to gain a powerful mind. Further continuing the practices, the mighty of that waves of the mind can be transferred in to power steps. If a person had been gained such an improved mighty in the mind, he will never chase the physical objects more than the quantity of his necessity. Because anyone doesn't carry the precious objects with his coffin. The lord Buddha's preaching had expressed, the luxurious life and the self-indulgence should have been omitted and strict physical asceticism also should be omitted. The middle way is the most precious for finding the Enlightenment. The rebirth is caused for sorrow, the desire is caused for the mind tension. Meditation against with desire, anger, and revenge can be caused to exponentially remove the mind tension.

Nirasha continually participated her lectures in university, and she gets her accommodation in the hostel of the institute. Within in the weekends she travelled to the home alone. But she didn't choose every weekend for visit her parents because of the burden of Tiran.

One bright afternoon in a miserable weekend, the time was around 3.00 p.m. Tiran and some of his friends had participated in a restaurant for a symposium that means a party organized by Tiran. Having a little chat, they started to discuss their plans. Mostly the main speaker was Tiran, and if there was a person with any opposite opinions, he will have to leave the group. The garbage is always collected with the large pile of same. Tiran had appointed some friends to spy about Nirasha's whereabouts. There were five young men with them. The majority of them were not involved with respectable employment. The party had been arranged in an urban restaurant. They started to sip the liquor. They gradually started to be talkative, but they didn't discuss any important thing, only boasting with obscene words. They didn't wanted to know about the important events because they were living in a distinctive darkness according to their knowledge.

The rest of them were continuing the oblation with more liquor. Tiran said, "I will never leave that bitch to be just freed from me, I will kill her whenever. I need your help to kidnap her." Podde said soon," I am always ready to help you, as you're my best friend, I can give you even my life, even Just now, let's go to take her. If you want, let's go right now." Then Kiththa said," You don't ever think about us with a doubtful mind, Tiran, we will never leave you in any kind of trouble with you". The emotions of their friendship had spilled with the glasses of liquor. Otherwise, they knew, Tiran was an avid alcoholic addicted person. These friends had been usually engaged for these free of charge liquor parties with Tiran, as he had spent lavishly for liquor. Therefore, many friends were being preferred to enjoy themselves with him.

"What do you say, give us the word, let's go now, don't be a coward guy", Kiththa challenged. Tiran enticed to do anything with his brave friends' utterances. "Okay! Now the time is 4.30 p.m. She usually comes home after nearly 5.00 o'clock. According to the information that I have received over the phone, she would be coming nearer in the town, definitely she will be walking along her path of the home. Let's start the mission now." Tiran's friends agreed. Gradually time passed. The glasses and bottles were rapidly finished.

While they were continuing the party, Tiran had a phone call from a spying man who was appointed by Tiran in the taxi hiring park. Some three-wheeler riders also helped to Tiran to be making the information of Nirasha. Tiran get the information about Nirasha over the phone. That three-wheeler rider named, "Sumith" said, "That girl, Nirasha just now got down the bus from capital city. She is about to searching a three-wheeler to hire, what can I do?" Tiran thought a while, and asked, "How many taxis are there in the park now". "Only two including mine", Sumith replied. Tiran said, "Don't let her to take a taxi, tell her you have another appointed hire, what is that other taxi is there in the park now?" Then Sumith replied, "It is one of a friend of mine". Tiran ordered, "Then call him to omit her hire soon, and let her to walk". Nirasha came toward the park and inquired about a hire. "I have an appointed hire, why don't you take a modern car from your father?" Nirasha came to other one and inquired about a hire to her home. But she disappointed and decided to walk her home. Sumith called back to Tiran and gave the details. By discussing with the friends, Then Tiran suddenly changed the early plan to catching Nirasha, and took a cool to Sumith. Tiran Said, "Sumith, take her in to your three-wheeler, and take her to a deserted way of that short cut of the bridge, go! go! And take her soon!" Sumith suddenly chased back of Nirasha. He stopped at Nirasha and said, "Miss, I have postponed my scheduled hire, now you can have your hire with me!" Nirasha was walking along the road in a very helpless moment, because the darkness had aroused at the time, she had to walk along about a 700 mts ahead to her home. The girl who had become a fear to walk alone, kindly accepted the invitation of that sinful and stupid sleuthhound. Sumith rode to ahead with Nirasha!

Sumith was one of stupid helpers of Tiran because Sumith had taken the permission to parking his three-wheeler by the political power of Tiran's father. He always helped Tiran's barbarian campaigns. Most of the three-wheeler riders involved illegal events such as transporting drugs, provides the space facilities to prostitutes in the passenger seat of the three-wheeler, some of them also use drugs, and conducting with drug dealers because I have seen such an event one day what I had experienced.

I went to the capital hospital one day because there was a hospitalized patient who had been lived near my home. While I was speaking with the patient in the ward, a familiar man who lived my area also had attended to the hospital. At the moment, I spoke with him and he said to me, I also could have return with him by having the transport facility of his three-wheeler. I had been gone to the hospital by common transport services because of the road congestion. Then I willingly agreed with him to travel by his three-wheeler. While we are travelling, he stopped and got off for a while, despite of me in the passenger seat. Within a few minutes, he returned with another person. That stranger was looked like a thuggery man, also got in to the three-wheeler and started to travel. While we are travelling, the rider asked from me to can I delay for about few minutes. Then I agreed because I couldn't have made any objection for them as I was travelling on free of charge. Then we turned to a river bank which laid on parallel beside the main road. They stopped the three-wheeler among some trees and started to be taken drugs. This is the first time ever I had seen a person how sucks heroine. I got down from it, and stayed away. I also was invited to take a shot of that unpleasant smoking, but I refused humbly. I already have gained a reputable and respective prestige in the community as a teacher, I never had taken such the dangerous and inveterately drugs. I am occasionally being used to take only a beer or some alcoholic liquor. After about 10 minutes, they finished the work. I saw a few small boluses of that drugs by wrapping with a thinner tissue with that strange man who got in to the wheeler on the way. I supposed, I should immediately keep off from these immoral people because if the three-wheeler will be faced to checking up from the police on the way, I also will be in guilty for transporting or allegedly possessed the drugs. Because supposedly that people may trap me about that offence. When we reached to the main road, I amicably get down and took a bus of common transport service.

✔ Tiran wanted to take a final decision about Nirasha whether she would like to marry him or not. Two friends among them wanted to release soon, they had implied that they have appointed another task or whether they willingly omitted those barbarians. Tiran, Kiththa and Podde hastily left the restaurant by Tiran's cab, and within quarter of an hour, they ambushed the way of that where the three-wheeler was riding with Nirasha. Sumith rode towards Nirasha's way and suddenly turned over to the shortcut. Nirasha shouted, "You have selected the wrong way! Stop! Please stop!" Sumith said, "Here is a shortcut, stay without shouting". Nirasha tried to jump out, but she was confined by the speed. Unexpectedly, Sumith raised the speed, and rode very fast, and within two minutes later, he stopped in front of Tiran's cab. The barbarians surrounded the three-wheeler! Nirasha was trapped by that wicked barbarians and dragged her in to the nearest thicket. She shouted, harshly struggled and bit the beasts disgusting hands. Finally, she was became into unconsciousness!

Usually, as on the other days, the sun was setting, the birds were flying to their nests, the evening dews were rising by inviting to a calm night, and the people were walking to their homes to be enjoyed that well-earned rest. Gradually the sun disappeared to let the spacious and cloudless sky to be accepted the full moon. Not for a crescent because that day was a completely matured time of the moon for this rural area. The water streams were usually flowing, the breeze was fluttering, the leaves and branches of the trees were waving, and the children were attending to the beds. The moon was impatiently waiting to peep because the sun was still rather sinking. The moon wanted to get in the sky to brightly shining with the blinking stars in the sky.

Prishan's grandparents had been waiting with a grate expectation for coming back their elder daughter to home, Nirasha who had left her studies at university for the weekend leave. But she didn't have to come back home at the usual time. Mobile phones were not introduced into this country during the period. My grandparents had guessed and decided, that Nirasha might have gone to the home of her friend or had been still accommodated in the hostel of the university, as she had used to spend little time according to the necessities of her studies. Then they had let the time. Without any information, my grandfather had gone to take a call to the hostel. There were the phone facilities in a nearer home. Then he had taken a call to the hostel and got informed about her leaving from the hostel. Then my grandparents had decided, Nirasha usually may have gone with one of her friends. Therefore, my grandparents hadn't gone to the police to complain about the disappearance of Nirasha. Although, my mother, Nirasha's younger sister has had a hidden doubtful feeling about this absence because Nirasha didn't have mentioned such a schedule to her early. The night passed quietly. My grandfather had gone to the post office with the purpose to be taken a phone call to the university. He couldn't have any clue about Nirasha over the phone. Then my grandfather had gone to the university. No one made information about Nirasha. She had participated in the lectures last morning, and she had left the university at about 3.30 p.m. My grandfather was rather disappointed and confused.

He had gone to the police station and had file a complaint. The police had informed my grandfather, to be inquired about the doubtful places, roads, and such people. They had inquired all of the places where Nirasha usually had been gone early. The police investigations were also started. No person, no any kind of information and no evidence. However, my grandfather had gathered some details, that the liquor party was held in the restaurant of Tiran, with Podde and Kiththa. My grandfather had also mentioned it in his police statement about it. But the police had expressed, that incident is much more usual because that was the routine of Tiran.

The investigative file of the disappearance of Nirasha was embedded in the deepest corner of the police cupboard. The complaint that made of Nirasha's father in the police also had secretly and gradually buried.
However, the villagers had harshly supported to be found information about her. Unfortunately, they could not find any kind of a clue. The time passed rapidly. Nirasha's family was embedded in a severe grieve and her disappearance infested their minds. Seconds were converted into minutes, minutes were converted into hours, and hours were converted into days, weeks, months, and years. Remains only an unbearable sorrow with my mother's family. My mother especially had ever suffered from her only sister's mysterious departure. They had been lived forever with the tears, after the incident. But they had a severe belief, that Nirasha wasn't dead. She will come to them whenever. The most important and fabulous event approached after a year of the disappearance of Nirasha.
Kiththa usually had taken a bottle of liquor and he had gone to find one of his friends. He wanted to enjoy with the friend. He reached to the relevant friend's place and had drunk both of them. After a few hours, the time was about 9.30 pm, Kiththa left the friend, and had ride his bicycle to return. About within half an hour, he was able to reach the mentioned bridge. He hadn't allowed to pass that bridge. The next morning, a farmer had been going to his paddy field and had seen the death body of Kiththa. He suddenly called the villagers and, they were to taken the proper action to inform it to the police.
The police had received information about this dead body. The dead body was defaced when it was found laid under a small bridge. But the police suspected it may be Kiththa's body, because the dresses and wristwatch matched and could identified. There was a foot cycle owned to kiththa. The postmortem about the body had revealed more information about the physical side of the death.
"Do you remember the small bridge, what is laid beyond about four km from our home on the shortcut?" Prishan asked me. I suddenly remembered the place as a flash, what I spent that time in a few years ago to have a clearer view of the surroundings under the full moon. If I were known about it, perhaps I might not stop my bike on that bridge. But according to my personal aspects, I always wanted to accept such dreadful challenges. Then If I were here at this time with the bike, I would have decided to ride my bike on the same way even this night. Because Now I extremely wanted to expose the mysterious enegma of Nirasha. Unfortunately, this time, I came here with Dinuj in his car to have participated in the funeral of Prishan's grandmother. I had left my bike locked in Dinuja's place. Then I should go with him to take my bike bypassing that mysterious way. Then I determined to search about the bridge later.
Kiththa was one of the accomplices who had committed as a partner in any kind of mischievous event of Tiran. He also had lived nearby the area of Prishan's home. He was being lived there at the time as a beast or as a disgusted person. He was a person like that, who can sale his entire soul only for a free glass of liquor. The file on the death of Kiththa was also gathered into hidden, mysterious, and unidentified homicidal file with piled up near Nirasha's corner of the police cupboard in the deepest place. The time incessantly had flown. The events had forgotten to the people with the time consumption. According to the postmortem report, Kiththa had died on a severe instant blood pressure with a heart attack. The forensic

medical officer had authenticated that decease had been happened on facing highly unanticipated terrible and dreadful event by the person.

Tiran had prodigally spent his money for the funeral of Kiththa. He wanted to show the community, he considerably treats his servants. He had donated some money to Kiththa's family. The organizing committee of the funeral management of Prishan's grandmother had to clear off the stuff what they had brought. Then the food tables had to clear, then we were invited for the dinner. Then we had to stop our discussion. There is a tradition in this country to provide free meals all of the participants for the funeral. Then we had to take the dinner. Having concluded the first bottle, we had opened the second. But we got dinner and intended to freely settle to start the discussion. The time was about 11.30 at night, Prishan also was tired and felt drowsiness. Then, we had to stop our discussion. We determined to be gathered at 7th day night of the death of his granmother, because there will be a donation for the Buddhist monks to be wished the posthumous soul of his grandmother. Then we also farewelled from Prishan and his family. I went to Dinuj's home with him for my night parking.

The next day I went to my home and involved my duties. But I bothered about the enigma of Nirasha in my mind. I thought the ways how did she disappeared without any kind of evidence? How her image does appeared me and spoke with me on the bridge? I have to explore about the ghosts and inhuman souls, how could they appear as an illusion and empowered to speaking with the people? I started to read and highly study about the ghosts, haunts and inhuman souls.

I found many fabulous and famous folktale and true stories of the ghosts. I studied about how had made the name of a rural village in this country.

That famous name of the village is, "Seventy knots".

The name of the village, seventy knots which is the semi-urban region located in a famous district for gems about 55 km far away from the capital city. There is a scary story originating in popular culture, typically passed on by word of mouth what is famous as a folktale. Already as you know, there were lived talented people in the world called "exorcists" who experts to handling the demons (devils), non-human spirits or ghosts by holding one's attention completely by bound spell chanting.

Long ago, there was a one of excellent charmers (hex) who had lived in that region. He had an ability to be tamed the devils and handle them to his own desire or preference by using his talents in exorcism. The non-human spirits when entered to the human body that means entered to the human body or mind by means of supernatural or levitating power of the demons. Those ascended demons can be repelled by the charmer which based on the demon's reincarnation.

The said hex lived with his young pregnant wife and they didn't have any early children because they were married recently. According to their family background, they didn't have any relations to care take the newly pregnant woman because of the charmer's terrible, mysterious and impenetrable performances. The exorcist frequently had had to leave his home for the exorcisms. While the hex was leaving out from his isolated home for the charms, the young wife was along in that had to spend loneliness as one has neither friends nor companions with her.

The hex was in a bigger trouble by leaving her alone because of her pregnancy, and designed a master plan as a strategy to be taken a servant for her assistance.

Although he could find such neither girl nor boy as a servant. Then the exorcist selected an inhuman monstrous devil and tamed him by immersing, which means embedding a charmed thorn in to devil's head as a little needle by using his talents in exorcism. But it was a very dreadful and difficult employment. Although, the exorcist decided to select such a boy's or girl's fresh dead body to charge a demon. While he was waiting on that intention, he had found an information about such a young boy's death who had died by drowning in a river. As he had planned early, he gathered an assistant to involve with this dangerous task. At the ancient era, there was not a manner to conduct a postmortem, an embalming or autopsy. Then the body was not with damages. When concluded the funeral, the body was entombed by the parents. Then at the midnight, the exorcist and his assistant stealthily reached to the grave yard with the early prepared stuff and exhumed the body and exorcist laid in the grave. After enchanting for two hours in the grave, with the relevant sacrificing rituals, the exorcist started to invite the relevant devils. There were appeared a few famous demons to be taken their victims. The said few famous demons were very dreadful and terrible. If there was any hesitation or delay for the appointed offerings at the punctual time of their appearance, the assistant or exorcist or both of them would have faced for very terrible events, even into the death. The assistant never must have looked the faces of those invited devils. The assistant could have conducted his duty successfully. The most terrible moment was the time that dead body was being recharged with an ascended inhuman soul. A hundred- and eight-times chanted thorn which early prepared by exorcist embedded into the head of the body for curb the soul. However, the exorcist and his assistant must have offered a requesting sacrifice to the ascended soul. Having accepting them, the body must have cleared with saffron liquid. After that the exorcist must enchant to tame the soul who ascended the body. The body should have been nominated with a new name. Unfortunately, that ascended soul was one of cruel and terrible haunts. But the exorcist had tamed him successfully. At the dawn, they went to exorcist's home.

After, every household task was being done by the said devil without being any disobeyed to the pregnant woman. The servant had adhered to be done all of the ordered workload by that pregnant woman, as an obedient servant. But, the true and real condition about the devil had been hidden by the hex from his wife. The assistant also was instructed by the exorcist to be protected the enigma.

One day the exorcist left out from the home for curbing another demon whoever levitated in to a human body. He had arranged all the prior vital necessities and started to spell binding. Meanwhile that the devil who had detained as a servant in the hex's home also heard that sound whichever how far away from the home he charmed. That was a typical aspect according to the exorcism. Unfortunately, the own home had not been protected that means the exorcist couldn't have protected his home that day before leaving, as doing usually by the hex. While he was leaving his home on an unanticipated event, he extremely had missed to take that precautious manner.

Meanwhile, the devil who was being served in the exorcist's home indicated, by showing the thorn to the pregnant woman by saying that was driven in to the head while he was finding the firewood in the jungle. The woman who expecting her first deliverance, had not informed early anything about the enchanted thorn, and she sympathetically dragged out it.

The hidden devil emerged and ascended to the boy suddenly, the hidden inhuman demon killed the woman and destroyed her matured embryo soon and left the home for revenge from the sorcery. The hex felt the incident on his excellent ability. Now he started to bind the spells with a yellow thread, he continually tied the enchanting thread to be caught the terrible devil's soul in to a tie. He had to enchant seventy knots to be curb the demon.

Finally, when chanting seventy knots, that the devil curbed. The place where the devil was curbed, at the seventy knots of the yellow thread was called, "Seventy Knots". That name is already used to be known that village.

I searched and found such the details about the more stories were based on true events about the ghosts and haunts.

Then I continually researched on such the hidden events are existed in this country. There were many stories have existed in the ancient kings, in the duration about hidden treasuries of the kings.

There was a hidden hoard of an ancient king under a huge stone. They had arranged to keep the significant symbols such as foot prints of the animals, swords, lotus flowers, crowns and thrones on such stone upon spaces to be identified and find the buried place of the hoard.

The kings had believed the inhuman souls, and had believed reincarnation of the people. Then they typically had selected a reliable man to protect that buried treasure trove and get promises him to ever dedicate to be protected them. At once, a hidden executioner who carries out a sentence of death on a nominated person by the king, does kill that person when he ended his oath. Meanwhile an exorcist who had fetched by the king is enchanting. The people believed such a person would ever be become a protector of that buried hoard as a ghost called genie, elf or gnome.

Such the buried hidden hoards at the past had been mentioned on the parchments that means a stiff, flat, and thinned which made of skin of an animal and used as a durable writing surface in ancient times by the kings. Such those parchments had been found in the ancient temples, museums and in the ancient palaces. Some people such as politicians, the government officials in the police department, the officials in the department of archeology and immoral, barbarian sons of the stupid politicians have dug these stones and had found the precious treasure troves in the present time. These people have taken the assistance of the delicate exorcists to be curbed the said gnomes.

Once, recently, there was a former famous and accused president for thefts, money laundering and stupidity in an unknown country and his foolish, cunning son had started to continually digging such the hoards during their tenure. They had used the political mighty to be dug the treasure trove with modern equipment. They had found many sources and had spent them to purchase the overseas lands and remains had deposited in such overseas banks. In this moment, as a repercussion of that stealing the governmental properties without being employed for the innocent people's prosperity, they are being refused by the people spitting even their names and photos. Among some of them, a least amount of lucrative people who secretly gained the unjustifiable advantages and the profits of that stupid former president and his son are still continually worshipping that beasts. But also, all the politicians who were invited for the TV programs frequently boasting, they are completely immaculate, perfect and principled. They express, they do have never involved with corruptions. These stupid and mendacious politicians and their governmental accomplices must be hit the seven lightings. The said unknown country is already faced into bankrupt position in this moment. The innocent people are being suffered in harsh poverty as the unaffordable heavy taxes on their lives. As my view, the politicians and the officials whoever collaborated for these crimes may ever strike lightning!

When unburied such the ancient hoards, a sacrifice should have been conducted to for the gnome to satisfy him. Because of the gnome is a legendary dwarfish creature that died person with willingly supposed to guard the earth's treasures ever in underground? That dwarfish soul may be appeared as a ghost or inhuman soul, probably as an animal or snake.

Once there had been reported a true story about trying to landing up a golden shrine. The details of the hoard been had received from an ancient inscription. A monk had found that inscription was being established in a cave type pagoda. The pagoda had made with an inner core and the people was able to walk or have the shelter in it. This pagoda was situated in an area which reserved as a world heritage property. The entire premises were being protected by the government. There had been deposited pure golden image, some golden coins and an ancient crown and ornaments of a former king and his queen consort as per that inscription had revealed. The said monk had found the details by studying that inscription, because it had been written in symbolized language. After confirming the language, and comparing the location, the details and aspects had been matched. The monk had a

combination with a powerful, talented, intelligent and young exorcist. They had studied the details and finally had been revealed, the gnome, which means the inhuman soul who had bounded with that hoard was a very dangerous demon. The demon should have been satisfied with only a victim of young **maiden virgin** as the sacrifice. The monk had a severely desire to be taken that hoard. He intended to take that property and after taking it, leave from the priesthood. He had been built an illegal intimate affair with an overseas woman. The monk had informed with her about that hoard in the pagoda. Then the woman severely compelled him to take the hoard any way. She had spent her money for the research of hoard.
Then the said monk started to find a maiden virgin for the sacrifice and launched a master plan for achieve it. The chosen exorcist also helped him.
Some poor young laymen in this country do leave their lay life because their parent's poverty. After they attended to the monastic life, they don't try to achieve the improvement of their concentration according to the religious leaders' philosophy. The path of the Enlightenment is the middle way by omitting that every desire such as lust, enviousness, anger, greed, animosity and covetousness. But also, in the present time, some of the priests who fulfilled with all corruptions do gather the physical properties rather than the laymen. Such the corrupted priests do preach to the politicians and both of the parties are being cheating the innocent people. Some priests do involve with prostitutes and use drugs. The corrupted priests and such politicians should have been shot and killed at sight, because they devastated the country and the religion. If such the immoral priests or politicians would be unable to protect their prestige, they should be left from their priesthood or leading the politics. Although some priests are being protected the priesthood properly and they will find their emancipation.
The said monk finally found a suitable girl for the sacrifice. The monk had a sibling brother was a handsome man. The monk persuaded him to the significant value of that hoard. Finally, he inclined to sacrifice his girl-friend who expected to marry recently. The sibling was assigned the liability to take her by deceiving her to inside the said pagoda. They had planned to take the hoard at a night time. The exorcist gathered all necessities for the sacrifice. The monk was always spying about the place by pretending the officials, that his time was being committed to studying and meditating in the pagoda. There were only two security officers engaging for the protection of the pagoda. The security officials who employed on the shift duties, by changing in a rotate system. There was a garrison nearby 500 meters of the pagoda, and never take any explosives to burst the treasure trove. Then they had to take the help of the security guard. However, one of them had cheated and caught for their tie. The monk had promised him to share a part of the hoard. Then they appointed a one Saturday night to take out the hoard. There were six partners for the hoard including monk and his overseas woman, exorcist, his assistant, monk's sibling and security guard.
The appointed Saturday evening, that the girl who intended to be sacrificed was invited by his boy-friend to visit an indoor musical show in the town area. He had taken two tickets early. The parents of the girl had released her to see the musical show with him.

The organizers of the show had early announced it will be started at 7.00 pm. The show started at the punctual time and clients enjoyed it properly. They had entered to the auditorium and while performing the show, the boy informed her about an urgent belly sickness of him and had to leave the auditorium. She happily had been participated for it and that boy had cheated her. The crew who were expecting the girl had planned to take her at the dark time. Then they had ambushed near the auditorium. When the boy and girl came out of it, a van with a monk and a driver had come and called to the couple to be dropped them. They pretended, now they have met randomly after a long time. The boy had introduced the girl to the monk as they are old friends of him. Then they got up the van. On the way, the monk had proposed to them, to have an essential appointed program with him and delay for a few minutes. The girl disappointed, because her boyfriend was suffering from a stomach ache. She asked about it, then suddenly the boy shut the girl's mouth. The crew caught her and they tied her hands and mouth. Immediately that driver who appointed by the exorcist, drove the van in to the pagoda. They had early prepared all stuff in the employed place, with extraordinary flowers, needed oil lamps, frankincense, incense sticks, candles, flambeaux and needed animals such as a goat and a reddish cock for sacrificing.

A suitable sacrificing bed for the girl had decorated with red flowers. The oil lamps and candles were lighted. The guard kept out of the pagoda for spying about the outside. The girl's dressings were taken off. It was not a vital compulsory, but the exorcist wanted to suffer her nakedness. He had bred an impatient lust like lovely emotion about her and at sight he decided to save her. Then he immediately changed his scheduled enchanting manner to taking the hoard. He initially enchanted for the protection of him, the assistant and the girl. But he didn't reveal about it with the others. They laid and tied her on the bed parallel. The sacrifice was started, at really 9.00 p.m. The exorcist and his assistant were busiest, the others were looking at the naked girl.

The exorcist started too charming. The assistant supported to the oil lamps to be continually lit and smoking with frankincense. The girl had laid on the bed tied her legs, hands, and mouth. The exorcist covered her eyes with a red kerchief and took a sword with his hand. He enchanted into the sword and started to invite the ascended terrible devil. The time was really at 12.00 pm. The girl highly tried to untie the hands. Then the exorcist ordered the crew to go back over 30 feet and stay there away. Then the crew got back about 30 feet. Then exorcist inaudibly said to the girl, “Don’t fear, and believe me! I will never allow to kill you by anyone! I promise with you, you will be ever protected with me! Believe me!” The girl scarcely accepted his word by shaking her head. Suddenly she was felt an unconsciousness condition. Then he called to the crew to be nearer with him. Exorcist continually charmed. A woman appeared and screamed, “I need my sacrifice, take me the goat soon!” Then hurriedly the goat killed by the exorcist. The terrible woman chuckled loudly and disappeared with the goat. Exorcist continued to charming and invited to the next demon. Then suddenly heard a terrible sound and cold breeze. Quickly appeared a devil with a trident, which means a supernatural creature.

He asked a cock. The exorcist killed the cock and offered it. He took the cock and disappeared. Then suddenly a man looks like a terrible devil with red eyes, elongated tongue and black fur came to the bedside and hooted three times and shouted, “I don’t need an innocent girl for my sacrifice, untie her soon and release her soon, untie her soon, untie her soon!!!” Then the assistant untied her soon. The exorcist highly enchanting and asked, “What do you want? Tell me soon!” tell me what do you want??” The devil terribly ordered, “I need that monk as my sacrifice!” The devil was gradually changed his appearance in to enlarging. The monk tried starts to run, but the sibling hugged him to be prevented his escaping. “Take him soon!” the terrible demon shouted again. Exorcist suddenly jumped on to the monk and killed him immediately by his sword! The dead body was taken by the demon and getting gradually become smaller and finally disappeared with the dead body. The exorcist believed the treasure trove will be emerge at the ending of enchanting, and he started to conclusion of the charms. Incredibly, there were another three hooting and immediately appeared another demon looks like a big black bear that hanging a long tongue with pouring the blood droppings. Its long claws and saber-toothed mouth were wetted with blood. The exorcist didn’t expect such an unknown devil and scarcely asked, “Tell me about your need!” The creature harshly groaned and aimed the boy. The boy also tried to run, but the assistant had more prior experience about such the sacrifices, if they will be unable to provide the requesting sacrifice to the gnomes, the assistant or exorcist should die for them. Suddenly assistant caught the boy and pushed him to exorcist.

Then the demon screamed, "Let that girl free, give her dresses soon, and offer her a part of the hoard, and promise me". "I promise, I extremely promise". Exorcist hurriedly offered the requested victim as the demon's request. The demon and the boy's body were disappeared soon. Exorcist continually charmed. Within half an hour, the girl restored and hurriedly get dressed.

Exorcist and the assistant had to persuade the girl that they are going to take the hoard. They dug the floor hurriedly and emerged the said treasure trove. The exorcist was a young, intelligent, smart and principled person, he divided in to four equal parts of the hoard. First part for the girl, second is for the exorcist, third for the assistant, and forth is for the security guard. The girl was dropped by the exorcist to her home with the wealthy sources. While on the way, the assistant asked, "Why did you ordered to us at that harsh dangerous time to leave you?" "I told a sweet secret with this girl at the moment", he proudly saw the girls face directly her innocent eyes and laughed. She looked at the exorcist to be offered her gratitude. Before long, and finally, there was a fertilized wedding with the girl and the exorcist. The exorcist was determined to ever stop his sacrificing activities after his wedding, because that hoard had given them an adequate and huge amount of money for their lifetime.

I further explored about an interesting and unbelievable haunting story had happened in a hospital. The hospital is situated in a rural area. It was a small one that conducted by a few staff including a young doctor, three nurses, a pharmacist, a camping officer for caretaker the sanitary services in the hospital and staff quarters. There was a separated building for mortuary. There were only three attendants, an ambulance with a driver, and a watcher. There were only two wards for male and female. A cooker and a helper had been appointed by the doctor for cooking the patients. All of them were paid by the government. Typically, the poor patients who had committed with stinging snakes, infected with fever or any other infectious illnesses, or any other type of injuring were attended to the hospital for medicating. The complicated patients were sent to the general hospital that situated in the main city. Long ago, the initial period of this hospital, had appointed a middle-aged doctor named in **Murthi.** Dr. Murthi had been working in this hospital for a long period about 25 years.

He actually was a very kind and sympathetic person for the staff and the patients. Then, he didn't have taken a transfer. In his period, there weren't any kind of complaint against for the hospital. Gradually the doctor was ageing. He was prepared for his retirement in the next two years on his old age. Then doctor Murthi who will recently allow to take his retirement, had successfully conducted the hospital. He extremely was an eminent person in the country.

He never had involved to private practices, and never sold the medicines to out of private pharmacies which provided by the government for the innocent poor people. On that condition, Dr. Murthi had found since a short time of recent period, which medicines were disappeared from the stores. There wasn't a storekeeper, that pharmacist had completely handled the medicines and the relevant documents. The doctor had received some complaints from the nurses about disappearing or scarcity of medicines. Then the doctor however stealthily made arrangements to take an inventory report of the pharmacy. He strategically taken the supplying reports that means goods receiving reports of the medicines from the general hospital to this rural hospital. The doctor patiently studied the goods issuing reports for about four months. He had been studied there was a large shortage of the medicine in the hospital pharmacy. His investigation had revealed a complicated theft of the pharmacist.

The doctor had launched a reliable person to spy who lived in the village to be gather the details about that pharmacist. The pharmacist had been often behaved near a large pharmacy of the town. He had hovered in the pharmacy for few times during the previous month. Doctor had early informed to the police about the event then, the doctor Murthi had informed to the relevant officials to check down the said pharmacy with the police assistance. In an evening, the pharmacist had entered to the said pharmacy with a bag. The spy had taken a call to the police and, then a respectable staff of officers of the health department and the police had raid the said pharmacy and had caught a significant number of medicines that disappeared from the rural hospital. The pharmacist and the owner of the large pharmacy had caught with the stolen goods. They were arrested by the police. Then finally that the pharmacist had to interdict from his service.

Before long there was a disciplinary investigation for the convicted pharmacist and, as a result of it, he was dismissed from the job. And he had to commit to imprisonment for two years.

The doctor's service had appreciated by the government and he was allowed to elongate his service for additional two years. He wanted to take his retirement but also, he unwillingly accepted that offering by the government. The doctor served in very enthusiasm way. The people who were treated by the hospital always praised the eminent service of the hospital. The number of wards had been increased to five and the staff also increased. The time had been consumed rapidly, that pharmacist who was committed to the imprisonment had released the prison as his punishing duration had concluded. He had fiercely sworn with his friends to revenge from the doctor. He had expressed with a hospital companion, "I will kill that man, if I will be unable to reappoint in the hospital as a pharmacist".

He wicked to make a plan for succeed it. He had launched a spying about the doctor. The doctor had informed about his furious utterances, although, doctor never had think, that person would be such an animalized person. The staff of the hospital also didn't have believed on his threatens.
Dr. Murthi continued his workload and he intended to definitely be taken his retirement after having completed the elongated additional period. He had planned to be abroad with his family after his employment. Because his daughter and son had been studied in an overseas reputable country. One night, at about 12.20 am, suddenly the power supply of the hospital was disconnected. Dr. Murthi was in the night duty at that day. Generally, the electricity supply is being disconnected in this country without the early warning. This weakness was a usual manner, because of the mismanagement of electricity board. The management of the electricity board and the politicians with top officials of the quality standards in the country are always being slept, because they were able to take their salaries instead of achieving the liabilities of the designation. The disgusting top officials of this country had used to work only if they would have any kind of underhanded beneficial in any duty. The power supply has been resupplied within about 15 minutes. There wasn't a power generator that fixed with automatically inaugurating system in the hospital. Unfortunately, Dr. Murthi had dead on his official seat in the hospital. According to the postmortem, that revealed the doctor's dead was a homicide. Because his neck had choked with a thin wire. An attendant had seen that night about 12.30 am, in the dark time duration, an unknown person who had worn a hooded black dress was leaving from the doctor's office room. There was the power supply with the surrounded buildings, then an attendant who was engaging on duty had checked the main switch board. The main switch had turned off position. He suddenly turned on it and had looked everywhere, to be known about what had happened. The unknown person had immediately disappeared. There weren't any kind of evidence except that attendant's statement. The police had to investigate continually. But the police were unable to find anything. A doctor named **Thudugala** who has newly appointed for the vacancy of Dr. Murthi,

accepted his duty, and also had chosen the former office room of Dr. Murthi. After about three months of the doctor Murthi's death, in one night, when Dr. Thudugala was in the office room about 12.30 am employed in a night shift, the new doctor had seen, another physician, who worn a neat and well-dressed, came to the office room and sat on the front seat of his table.

While the newly appointed doctor was in a nap of his seat, he slightly had seen that was an old gentleman looks like Dr. Murthi. The person who sat on the front seat had said, "I think, Dr. Thudugala doesn't know about me, because we didn't have meet before, I want to talk about something with you! Then Dr. Thudugala allowed to him, "Yes, tell me your problem?" "I am going to talk with you about Dr. Murthi's death! Would you please help me?" the stranger asked. "Yes, why not! I always ready to find that crime", Dr. Thudugala replied. "Then Doctor, please can you search and find, that there will be a necklace on that cupboard, then please don't touch it with your bare hands, because it is the murder's necklace of Dr. Murthi. You can observe it with the police officials and take the DNA samples of its spreading, because the necklace had scratched the murder's neck while it was pulling of the murder's neck. Definitely, I know the owner of it was former pharmacist of this hospital!" Dr. Thalagala wanted to know the name of that instantly appeared stranger. "Who you are Mister?" he asked. Suddenly the stranger stood of his chair and slowly left the room. A little cold breeze came to the room. Dr. Thudugala also stood and checked everywhere, but he couldn't find any person.

Next morning, the police came to the hospital according the phone call of Dr. Thudugala and found the said necklace that was on the said cupboard. Dr. Thalagala enthused to recognize the stranger who came to his office room, and well-studied the photograph of Dr. Murthi and identified, that person who gave the information about the necklace is Dr. Murthi's inhuman soul! The former pharmacist had immediately arrested by the police and got tendered to a test. According to the result of DNA test, they correctly matched with the former pharmacist. He was caught with the evidence and he later had made a self- confession how he killed Dr. Murthi. At that miserable day when Dr. Murthi died, the said pharmacist had stealthily entered to the hospital and was staying by hiding in a secret place of the office room for half an hour and when Dr. Murthi came to his office room from the ward, The doctor had sat down on his armchair, and started to study about the patients reports. Meanwhile, the former pharmacist had turned off the main switch to be disconnected the main power supply. The doctor had lit a little pen-torch. Suddenly, the murder leapt on the doctor with an early managed wire and wrapped around the doctor's neck. He highly choked the doctor's neck. Doctor harshly tried to loosen it and fought against him. Then the necklace of the wicked pharmacist had tightly restricted with the doctor's fingers. Doctor had suddenly thrown it on to the cupboard before a very nearest moment of his death. The cupboard upon layer was a rather high about six feet. The necklace didn't have found anyone at his postmortem. The murder also didn't have had any idea about the necklace, because an attendant was coming toward the doctor's room with a lit candle. Then the murder had escaped. The police had taken a legal action of the murder, and have been able to completely prove the homicide that didn't have given the benefit of the doubt of the murder. The accused pharmacist had punished to penal servitude for the lifetime.

I furthermore explored the famous haunting stories that were obviously known the citizen. One day I had to participate in a party that had been arranged by a friend of mine. The friend had selected to a scholarship in an overseas prestigious university for three years study course. Then his companions arranged a farewell party for him. Then I also was invited by them. I reached the appointed restaurant at the punctual time. Having completed the welcome speech by the organizing committee, the participants were invited a symposium. Then we altogether had some liquor and started to chat. While the conversation, I wanted to gather some details about the haunts because I have been following such stories relative for Nirasha's haunting event on the bridge in that time duration. Then I amicably pulled my topic about the subject. Then my friend named **Nalaka Galagedare** who was recently expecting to leave the country also started to narrate his own experience. He was working as a sight engineer in a construction project of a reputable company.

He had to work from 8.00 am to 5.00 pm in that site. He had been accommodated in a rented apartment by the company. He was provided a nice four-wheeled power steering jeep to be travelling to the worksite.

That working project was situated about four km far away from his accommodation. Because the site was established in a wilderness area. The workers with a supervisor were accommodated in the site where made a temporary hut made by galvanize sheets. They prepared their meals in the site kitchen. As the site engineer, he had to take all the responsibilities of the site. It was established in rather among some mountains, as the project had to assign made a huge water tank. Sometimes, he had to work more hours in the site according to the appointed workload for the day. There was a burial ground on the way of his travelling. So many rumors had established among the villagers about this burial ground. Although he doesn't care about the haunts or inhuman souls. One day, he worked for long hours. A reliable worker had hunted a wild boar about 7.45 pm, and they had convert it to pork within one hour. My friend, the site engineer was drastically preferred to eating pork crackling as the bite with liquor. Then he also offered some pork to be made a fried curry of pork. The servant told him, "Sir, there are two parcels of pork. The big one is for you because it is porkier. The small one is contained the unwanted pieces of meat." He asked, "What is the reason that second one is given me?" The servant said' "The first one has protected by the inhuman souls by inserting a few iron nails, second one may be wanted you to offer them to anyone who concerning about the meat". The engineer couldn't understand his puzzle. The engineer asked, "Tell me the reason, why should I take this wastage with me". The servant said, "If someone may request the meat on your way, loudly say some hard abusive words and throw this parcel onto his face!" "Okay, now I got the idea!" Suddenly he remembered an incident previously that he was faced on the way at night near the grave yard, but he didn't explain that incident at the moment. He had a cook to be made his meals who appointed by the company. He took a phone call on his cook and informed him to take a bottle of liquor before close the wine stores and get ready with other provisions to make a pork curry. Then he took that pork parcels and detained it in the jeep. He had to release the site about 9.00 pm. He wanted to reach his accommodation soon, before the cook leaving the apartment. Usually the cook doesn't leave the apartment until the engineer's arrival. He started the jeep and drove fast more than the other days. While he is reaching the burial ground, he saw a woman is there on the middle of the road with a small child. He could evidently look them on his powerful headlights.

They had worn rags and didn't have used even a comb with their grown hair. Usually, he doesn't have any fear of haunts because of he actually had known, that fearless and brave persons cannot catch the inhuman souls. He stopped the jeep in front of that woman and child. "What do you want", He asked loudly. The woman said, "My son very much prefer to eat pork with raw blood, I need the parcel that you have separated for us!" Then suddenly, he threw the small parcel to them. They disappeared soon. He had used some abusive words to them, "You don't appear for me again b..., f....bitch!" He doesn't have any hesitation to face the haunts and he expected to meet them regularly.

Then we wanted to know about the other incident which he had experienced on that way. He explained also that event. "One day, the site workers had cooked an iguana meat curry in their kitchen. They asked me to have a dish for me with my lunch. I also prefer to eat them allowed to keep a dish. The curry was very tasty and delicious. I ate it greedily. In the evening about 6.30 pm, I left the site to travel into my apartment. I drove the jeep along the way, but I didn't try to drive fast. Really in front of that grave yard I saw a black and big something running towards the jeep on the way. I could see it very clearly and closely looks like a black bear. I didn't slow down the jeep and increased accelerate. The creature crashed on my front buffer and was thrown away. I was sure as the crashing sound and shocking beat was felt me. Then I stopped the jeep and got down with my torch light. I saw something on my torch light was tried to frighten me by hoisting his hands. I saw an unbelievable event. There was a man with black hair throughout the body and with two saber toothed besides its mouth. His eyes was reddish and brighten. I tried to quickly hit him with my torch. The man was quickly disappeared. I understood that was only an imagination." He stopped the narration and took an else shot of his glass.

Then, there was a retired military officer in the group. He also explained his previous experience about a haunting story during had happened in the battlefield at the war time. There was a racialism conflict in the country for 30 tears. Many influential countries had involved to catch fire for this conflict, because they had received the lucrative benefits by selling air crafts, weapons and ammunitions to the both sides. Then the influential countries didn't interfere settle the conflicts of the developing countries. The immoral politicians of the country doesn't take a proper action to stop the war by implementing a satisfied constitution of the racialism. The short-sighted basted politicians of the both nations had deceived each other. The young sons or daughters of the innocent poor people of the country who involved the war that both nations, had to dedicate their lives. The politicians and the war leaders of both sides were getting benefits of armory transactions. The peace discussions had been launched by the government. Therefore, the both side had been agreed to implement a truce. During the truce, all combats had been stopped temporary. In one night, the time was about 2.30 am, the terrorists had unexpectedly started to attack the regiment. The officials or soldiers never expected to fight during the truce. But the terrorists had violated the conditions of the truce. The camp was established at verging a beach side and other side was covered with a thicket. There were bushes and with grassy land. The garrison had covered with a few protective bangles with some small barracks around the camp. Main garrison was sheltered by that barracks. There were 350 soldiers and 34 staff officials in the garrison. As he explained that, "I was a cadet officer in the camp. I had to cover the main garrison. The commanding officer and all the officials also were being involved for the combat. The terrorists had started to attack the first bangle of the camp. The soldiers didn't hesitate to counter-attack. We had bravely faced for the attack successfully.

We launched the very highly powerful weapons to repel the terrorists. There were loudly bursting sounds. The combat was held about two or three hours. We had to take the help from our air forces by sending the messages through our head-quarters. Then about 5.30 am, the area was become a soundless calm condition. We gradually checked all the area to find the casualties of our soldiers, whether had injured or died. We could find about 25 injured soldiers and eight dead bodies in the camp site. Having ensured the garrison and the camp site, we checked the outside of the camp premises for find the enemies. They had buried the mine bombs. We had to search the area very carefully. We could find 84 dead bodies of the enemies. There was a very clever corporal in our camp named, **"konne"** among the victims who also had to offer his life in this conflict.

He was a talented sniper. He had the ability with shooting in the darkness at his target very correctly. Otherwise, he was an honest soldier and loved the country. Corporal-Konne Kinsam was appreciated by all the officials and soldiers as his humble and amicable behavior. His unexpected farewell was a huge loss of our regiment. The time was passed, the camp also refilled the crew for the shortage. After a few weeks, at a one night, the commanding officer was there in the garrison and usually, we had established the protective strategies. At about 9.30 pm, a strange soldier directly appeared in front of the commanding officer and made the usual reputation. He has appeared as a familiar soldier in to the camp, and had told, "Sir, there will be launched a huge attack against for this camp to night. The terrorists already are being oriented this camp and travelling about 12 km far away from the camp. It is a huge enemy forces. Get ready soon!" The soldier had turned back and suddenly disappeared. The commanding officer couldn't identify the said soldier. But that soldier's face was familiar to commanding officer, although he couldn't recognize him. However, the commanding officer had called an urgent meeting with the officials and immediately launched the auto-activated drone camera technology to spy whether the information that given by a strange soldier is true or falsehood. We could see a huge enemy force including with about 600 soldiers with huge and powerful weapons are being rounded the camp on our computer monitors. Then we informed the head-quarters and requested the help. They called us, and ordered to get ready and enforce the front protective bangle. The air-force also informed to get ready for face this unanticipated event. The air-force sneaking and spying silent pilotless helicopters also had employed to be hovered in the sky and could find a huge force is being travelled towards the camp on the land and in the see. The enemy forces had selected the sea side and thicket to safely reach the camp. They had only remains to half an hour time duration to start the firing. Suddenly, our air-force had launched a huge, unbearable and very terrible attack with the powerful missiles to the enemy's battalions. Within about a one and half hours, the air-force informed us that the enemy forces had been devastated on the spot. If the said huge terrorists' brigade unexpectedly surrounded the camp or entered the camp, we will be unable to freely employ our air power as we would have to stop or restrict the air attack because it can be drastically harmed to the camp. Although, no one faced any kind of trouble in our camp.

All the post investigations were conducted within three days. The investigation showed and reported about 469 dead bodies and huge numbers of weapons, four war tanks had been devastated by the air attack of our forces.

The next event was paying attention to investigation about the soldier who appeared that night in front of the commanding officer and how he gave that real information. The commanding officer immediately called a parade and questioned all the soldiers and officials about the said hidden soldier. No one answered. But a friend of Konne said, "Sir that died soldier, Konne at the previous attack appeared me suddenly that evening and said me to get ready for a fatal combat! I wanted to speak further with him, but he suddenly disappeared!" The commanding officer get bring Konne's photograph soon. He checked it and identified that the soldier who suddenly appeared and given information. Then the commanding officer decided to be built a monument for Konne. His rank was uplifted.

SERGEANT KONNE KINSAM
1993- CODWALL GARRISION

That konne,s monument still can be seen in the front yard of that garrison." The retired military officer concluded his narration, and took his glass.

I was able to find another fabulous story from a rural suburban village. The village was located in a remote area far away from capital city of the country. There were more agricultural lands when harvested period, the farmers had sufficient money. Common transport service was scarce into that village after at 7.00 pm. as the road had been broken due to the ill-maintained. The drivers didn't liked to drive on that way because of the buses and other vehicles had been approached to the accidents on mostly break downs by falling the huge pits on the road. The farmers had been frequently requested the government to repair the road. Then the farmers finally had understood that the deaf governors won't make the road. The passers of the road had to travel on foot or the own private vehicles after that time. A few people had faced the same type of burden because of a haunt at a deserted area. The haunting burden had drastically infested to the night time travelers. The haunts usually had robbed the victims when they became afraid the haunt. The incidents had informed to the police and it has reported in the newspapers. A journalist was there living a nearby village, had to participate for investigate and compose an article for his newspaper about this haunting event. He decided to visit the village and explore about the haunt. He usually carried a camera and other stuff with his back sack. The young journalist didn't revealed with the villagers, about the real reason why he had to visit that village. He never believe in the haunts, ghosts and inhuman souls. He was a young, brave, and talented sportsman and had highly practiced martial arts. Then he went to that village in the evening time and gathered more details about the poverty and the other burning issues including the broken road. He unnoticed the reason he actually come for. He gathered the details of the haunt that was been bothered the passers of the way at night time. He deliberately delayed his returning because he wanted to know and face a said haunt on the way. He took his motorcycle at about 9.00 pm. for return. While he was riding the bike, he had to ride it very slowly because of the hardness of the road. Suddenly, he could see a very height man, that high was extraordinary. His height was about 8 feet. Although, typically the average high of a man of this country is about in 5.6 to maximum is in 6 feet. Then the journalist identified, this is the said haunt. He had a little fear, but he had guest early as that the received details, the haunt can be a trick for rob the people. The haunt came to him and he stopped the bike. He could see the on his headlight, a bloody face and reddish hands of the haunt. Haunt had worn a cloak. The haunt frantically laughed to be got the terrible sound and tried to frighten the journalist by hoisting the hands. But, the journalist very quickly got down the bike and kicked the haunt's chest side very powerfully. The haunt shouted loudly and fell down. There were two people in the cloak one on top of another. Then the journalist kicked the others face and finally, could surrendered them. He had caught a first man harshly. He had ordered the second man to tie him with a tree. Then journalist had tied the first one with the tree. Then he had called the villagers and had taken a few photographs of the tied people. The villagers identified the persons who appeared as a haunt. There was an exorcist in this village. He doesn't really practice the subject and didn't have sufficient knowledge about exorcism. This fake exorcist had collected an assistant also didn't have suitable knowledge of exorcism. Their activities on the subject always had failed. They wanted to increase their business. The exorcist had made a plan to frighten the people and after the scare of victims could bring to involve his remedies. According to his purpose succeeded, the person who committed in mental weaknesses on that hauntings could charge them to huge amount of money for his fake treatments. The exorcist was sat on the assistant's shoulders and worn a cloak. A kind of juice with red color plants had used for pretending as blood. According to the victims mental position, if the patient in completely scared and became to unconscious condition, they had robbed the patient. The newspaper that the journalist was being worked at the moment had proudly reported the headline about the haunt trapping mission. The fake exorcist and his assistant had arrested by the police.

There was another story about a deceased woman who committed a very miserable event in a coffin. While reading or hearing about her unfortunate event in her coffin, someone may never be believed this story. Although, this is exactly a true story. When I was a student in the primary school of our village at that moment, I was really ten years old in 1986. My mother was a nurse in a government hospital. She authenticated this story, because she had seen this deceased female body. She described this story with us. At the decade of 1980, there was not an improved medical treatments for the patients in this country who had died on stinging the snakes. A women who was about 35 years old had gone to the jungle to be collected some firewood with her son. She had collected some firewood. Accidently, she was committed to snake bite. That means she was stung by a cobra. The son immediately shouted to adults and take her to the home. There wasn't a nearby hospital. Usually, when someone was bitten by a snake, the victim was medicated by a rural physician. There was an experience physician in their village. The patient was lodged in the physician's infirmary. Unfortunately, the patient was died within three days. Generally, there was a traditional idea, or option among the people such a dead body that victim to die on snake biting should have bury in a blackboard wooden box and they never embalmed such a body. That tree can be defined as Alstonia scholaris or devil's tree in English is an evergreen tropical tree in the Dogbane family. It was a belief of the ancient people, if the dead body of such snake biting deceased was buried in a blackboard wooden box would be approached the rest of peace. The dead woman's coffin also made of that wood. In addition, the all jewelries of the woman had used in living should have been deposited in her coffin. This tradition was mostly considered the relatives and adults because they believed, if the deceased woman had a harsh desire for them in her lifetime, her inhuman soul will be return to the home that she was lived and will be bothered to the relations. According the all of these traditions, the coffin was buried within two days of her death. The grave yard was established in a deserted area. Having being completed her funeral, the relations and neighbors were withdrawn. The deceased women had used a considerable and valuable amount of jewelries in her life time. These jewelries also will be buried with her. An unknown person had participated for her funeral. He presumably counted the value of that jewelries. He planned to secretly unbury the jewelries. But also, he should have taken them before putrefaction of the body. Then he gathered a reliable companion as the supporter in the burying mission. They reached to the grave yard at about 12.30 am, and very meticulously searched the surroundings. A watchman had been employed the graveyard. He may detain in the graveyard till about 1.00 am. Typically, such the graveyard watchmen leave the graveyard, after 1.30, as they were not supervised by any authority after at that time. The unknown person and his helper were looking by hiding beside the yard. They had frequently experienced that watchers definitely may leave the graveyard after approximately 1.00 or 2.00 am. As their expectation, the watcher left the graveyard about 1.30 am. Then, they inaudibly started to dig the grave. They heard some dogs ululating at the village, then they guess that watcher is still going to his home.

Within about in an hour they were able to pose the coffin. They slowly opened the coffin. The grave diggers were jumped out of the pit. Because, the body had turned to other side, that means knit wise position. The supine body which means the anticlinal body had turned downward. The man who has participated the funeral exactly saw the body was purl wise there in the coffin. He surprised about this convert. Then he get confirmed, is that the woman whether had died or alive at the moment. He authenticated the woman had died at that moment. Then, what could have happened to the body? They suddenly checked the body, were there the jewelries with the body. There were all buried things as they were in the coffin. The grave digger collected them and kept them into his bag. They hurriedly and slightly closed the coffin lid and left the grave yard.
The next time, at the time of rising the sun, the watcher came to the graveyard. He looked the grave had dug and didn't have closed it properly. Then he got scared and hurried to close the coffin. Suddenly he heard a fine moan beneath from the coffin. He quickly ran to the road and shouted the people. Some villagers suddenly came to the grave yard and opened the coffin. A fabulous event! The woman was alive. Then initially people didn't closed her. Although the relatives also had quickly known the incident and come to the coffin and searched the body. The woman was not dead! She was very quickly hospitalized. The doctors had hurriedly treated her and saved her. According to highly committed medical investigation, there had been revealed, the wood that blackboard tree had activated to absorb out her snake poisonous gasses from her blood during two days. The night that she was buried, the poisonous gasses absorbing process of the wood had been highly activated. The woman had gained her consciousness and tried to come out of the coffin. Then finally, she was hardly able to turn other side. Fortunately, that grave digger had opened the coffin at the punctual and lucky time of the woman.

While I was surfing the stories about ghosts and haunts, I found a fantastic funny story about a devil. This humorous story is exactly not true. This is a fictitious story. There was an ugly middle aged man. His teeth were established irregularly by birth. Those were not stood in a same line. Some were protruded inside and some were outside. Extremely ugly. His old parents were in grieved about this unnatural establishment. He didn't ever have any girlfriend as this abnormality. Then he was compelled to be submitted by his parents to a clever dentist. The dentist made his teeth properly with a few operations within six months. But they had to spend a considerable amount of money for that. After having the proper shape of the face and teeth, he was able to marry a same aged woman recently. He had rather a foolish unmarried old friend with same position of only three teeth established irregularly. That foolish friend had gone his relatives place for a suitable job for about two years. He had to work for two years there. When that friend return to the village after two years, the teeth were improperly established man had made his teeth very beautifully and properly. One day, they had gathered and were having a drink, that foolish friend asked, "How did you make your teeth such a nice way, can I also make my bad teeth as yours?" The next man said, "Why not? You also will be able to make your teeth very nicely like me" he answered. Then he wanted to know that way how could he also make his teeth from his friend. Meanwhile, they became harshly intoxicated. Because their bottle had empty. Then the friend who only three teeth existed improperly asked again, "Please tell me guy, how did you make your teeth properly?" The first man wanted to make a kidding him and told, "One day I had a party with a gang of my friends and drank much. We were provided nicely fried pork for the bite. That fried pork was very delicious. I had never ate such tasty pork.

I ate them well. When the party was finished, I had to return alone on foot through the grave yard in our village. At the time about 12.30 am, I was suffered a very deep sleepy near at the grave yard. Then I found a nice tomb and I slept on it. In the next morning, when I was get up, I felt a very strange of my teeth as they were properly established. Then I looked surroundings, I saw a man was sitting nearby me. Damnation! There was a dreadful devil with me. He was harshly crying! "Why do you crying here?" I asked. The devil said "I am sorry my dear friend, I was suffering from a severe starvation as I didn't have a proper diet for three days, then I tried to detach the stuck fried pork pieces with your teeth that remains through your teeth. But with on my hasty, I had detached your teeth and I wanted to attach them, as soon as the previous position. But you were being got up. Then I rearranged them improperly. I am sorry brother! But the devil couldn't understand that was the proper way I wanted to keep my teeth. Then I told to the devil, don't worry about that arrangement." The devil said, "I am the care-taker of this grave yard, if you want any kind of help, you can come to this place and call me!" Then the devil disappeared soon, because his wife devil had called him soon.

That foolish old friend had believed that kidding. He had arranged a fried pork and adequate liquor. He finished the bottle halfway at his home. After he went to the graveyard about 11.30 pm, and started to continue the drinking. He was suffering from intoxicate and slept by expecting well-managed line of teeth. The first day, he couldn't achieve his target. He thought, that devil may have taken his day off at that night. He came also in the next night. But he couldn't achieve his purpose. He came for three nights into the grave yard. He will never meet such a devil in that place.

There was another haunting story with a young man named **Nikhila.** A newly married couple had lived in a suburb. Before their marriage,they had employed in a governmental office, when they were working in a same office, had been built up a love affair. The young man worked as an assistant manager and the young woman had been working as a clerk. The man had granted a quarter for his accommodation to living in it during their working period. His name was **Nikhila.** His wife was **Erandika**. They happily lived for a long time but also, they didn't have the kids. They had consulted more gynecologists and furthermore had taken the instructions from the invisible forces such as deities, exorcists and the religious bodies. But also, they haven't been able to take any help to resolve their problem. Erandika doesn't have the fecundity. The relations, neighbors and official friends had been mocked them about their failure. The time was gradually flown. Erandika had an elder brother named **Priyanka** always visited his sister. He had a beautiful wife named **Ahinsa.** Extreamely she, Ahinsa was a very nice sexy woman who could enchant anyone. Her actions, her behavior, and her gaiety that means her working style were attractive and sexiest.

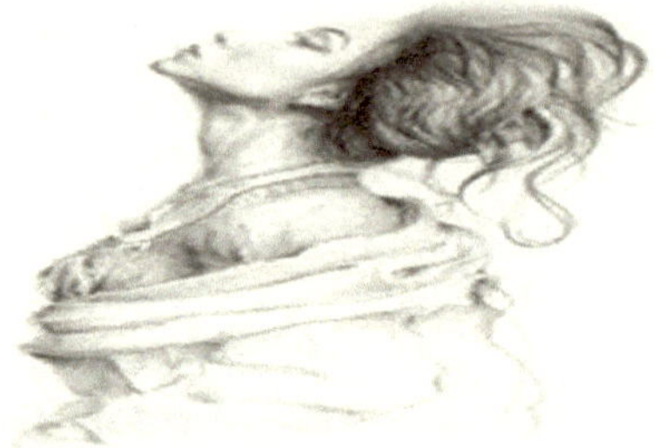

Ahinsa also often came to visit Erandika. While they were being become to friends instead of the relationship, Ahinsa's husband, Priyanka became to a reliable friend with Nikhila. They were committed to going trips, more excursions and gathered in every festive times. Nikhila usually an outgoing person, he always arranged a liquor party when they were gathered in the home. Before long, Ahinsa was pregnant. During this period, Priyanka had to leave the country, because he had early applied a foreign employment. He had early settled the expenses for the journey, with job money and air tickets. Then he was unable to refund the money, because there was a bond that paid amount won't be reimbursed in any kind of reason. He had to take a sum of money from Nikhila and Erandika on a loan basic to be settled that expense. "What to be done?" Priyanka said and got ready to leave the country by adapting his mind, for a better future of their family and the expecting child. Ahinsa hadn't any other help except Nikhila and Erandika. Then, Priyanka decided to detain his pregnant wife with Nikhila and Erandika for more shelter. Erandika willingly accepted her and took the permission of Nikhila. Before long, Priyanka left the country and Ahinsa settled in Nikhila's home. After his departure, he had written a few letters to Ahinsa.

While Priyanka working in an overseas farm owned by a kind foreigner, he wanted to send some money to Ahinsa. Because there was a large owning with them and had to immediately settled. Then Ahinsa requested from Nikhila to take a call of Priyank's boss and to be asked for three month salary advance. Then Nikhila had explained the poor and critical condition of Ahinsa and Priyanka with that boss. The said boss had promised with Nikhila to care take Priyanka as a brother. Nikhila is able to speak in English fluently. Then Priyanka was able to receive an advance as the boss was a very sympathetic person. Despite such a kindness boss, Priyanka didn't satisfy to work that place, because his stupidity. Priyanka had been able to meet a local friend who had met early in this country. That friend had promised to Priyanka for refer him to a new job at a very high salary than the job he was being entered by his agency with that eminent boss. Then Priyanka had escaped from the working place without having his documents and the passport. Unfortunately, Priyanka didn't have found such an over-paying employment as his friends promise. The friend was a racketeer, he had taken a considerable amount of money from Priyanka to convey him a profitable recruitment. As Priyanka had given the money to that friend, he had left the currently working place. But, he couldn't find the friend because he doesn't know the language of the country. He didn't have learnt how to speak in English. Then he was disoriented in that country and was situated far away from his own country. Finally, he had arrested by the police as he didn't have his passport with him. He was detained in that country for a few months as a refugee. That was the reason he didn't write to his wife.

Nikhila and Erandika usually leave from the home in the morning about 7.30 am. They prepared their meals early in the morning, and took with them for breakfast and lunch. They usually returned home at 5.30 pm, having completed their daily duties. They detained at home only in holydays. Ahinsa worked in the home at the daytime. The time watch was rapidly rotated. Sometimes, Nikhila was treated by Ahinsa if Erandika was busy for making tea and offering them. Ahinsa had a fantastic and enchanting sexy body.

Akhila usually tried to stealthily look at her nakedness while she was bathing. They didn't have a fully covered bathroom. He cared to be done these unethical peeping while she was changing her dresses in her room. He looked at Ahinsa in a lust-like emotion. He desired and wished to be seen if Erandika also with pregnancy. Gradually, Nikhila was become an over-enthusiasm of Ahinsa. He always thought about Ahinsa to take his capture. But he didn't hurry to imply his emotion to her. He strategically implied her to his enthusiasm. One day, when Erandika was in the yard, Nikhila asked from Ahinsa, "I also like to be a father, whenever please can you consider to give a birth of mine child in your womb?" Ahinsa had never thought and expected such a peculiar suggestion. She never wanted to kick off her benefits of Nikhila's home. She may have supposed, this man is very eagerly expecting an own baby. But also, there is an obstacle for it with his wife's bodily weakness for conceiving a baby. Although, Nikhila may have thought her about sexy figure. One evening, Nikihla wanted to express his desire of Ahinsa. He stealthily painted a lovely heart mark and wrote on it, "Ahinsa, I love you Baby" on his palm and showed it to Ahinsa. She looked at his palm and smiled beautifully. Her smile was able to reveal that, she will never betray him to anyone about this message. Then Nikhila understood, Ahinsa doesn't have any kind of opposition of his love. He decided firmly, Ahinsa will never reveal his mad behavior with anyone. Then he decided to write about his restricted concepts in his heart. Before write that, he thought more times about her and finally wrote her. At the night time, while Erandika and Ahinsa was sleeping, Nikhila wrote an emotional love letter to Ahinsa. He wrote it very nicely.

Dear Ahinsa, 1995.07.05

I will never have been understood why I was allured to writing such this letter for you dear Ahinsa. I am already suffering with an attractive and lovely concept about you. I have approached in a firm mentality about your loneliness because, this is the most important time duration that your husband closely should have been with you. Although, you have deprived that fortune. I am bothering to replenish that shortcoming with you. Because of I am unable to look away when you suffer and my sympathetically concept that has emerged about you in my mind. Why don't you allow me to help you? Please don't be fear, I will never reveal with anyone about it. If you would like to closely love me, I would protect you as a precious gem. Your child should have grown with a father's shelter. In case, Priyanka won't come back for you, I promise you, you will never be allowed to disorient with my love. If you want to betray me to my wife or with your husband, you will have to departure from my eyes. You can have a free decision to hand over this letter to my wife or your husband whenever he would return. Unless, you can start to write a lovely life story with me. I will be a real father for your child. Then shall we write a new, lovely and fantastic life story named with "Nikhila and Ahinsa?"

Your unchanging lover, Nikhila.

The letter handed over to Ahinsa in the early morning while Erandika was cooking in the kitchen. She read it soon and hide it under her pillowcase. Ahinsa had to visit lonely for her monthly medical clinics, because her deliverance had reached at the near future. Nikhila considered to travel with her for those medical clinics with her. During their travelling, Nikhila had willingly pretended to the health officers as the husband of Ahinsa. However, Ahinsa had given a birth to male baby. The boy child and Ahinsa also lived in Nikhila's home. After the birth of the child, one day Erandika had to leave the home in a holyday for her essential duty. Then Nikhila had amazed and planned to touch with Ahinsa such a day. In the evening, about 2.00 pm, the child was breast fed by Ahinsa on her bed. She looked at the wall side while the child feeding. Nikhila inaudibly sat up the bed and leant her back and kissed her neck. She closed her eyes and savored the taste of his finer kissing. She pretended that she was rather in a nap, then didn't opposed to him. He turned her to his side. Nikhila request to be calm her. "What do you want, I am feeding my baby", she muttered. Nikhila requested her to allow also him to feeding. Ahinsa allowed him. He closed his eyes and fed by her breasts and savored the taste. The baby was sleeping. He lifted up her and took her into his bed room. Ahinsa asked, "What are you going to do, in case Erandika would come now?" "Please don't try to stop me", Nikhila said.

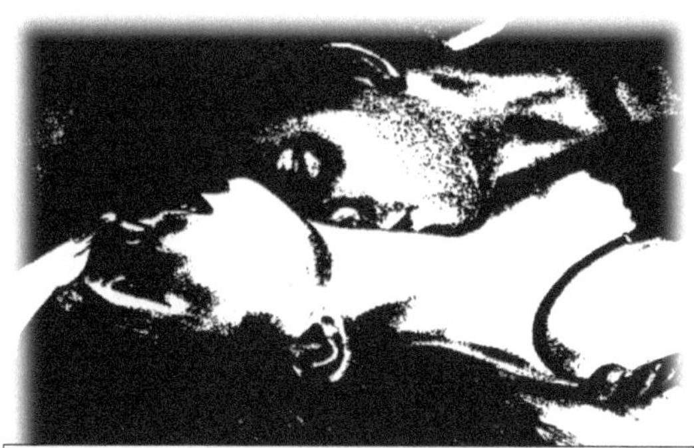

He started to kiss her neck, suck her lips, cheeks, breasts, and her pointed nipples. Gradually ....!

He laid her on the bed and fell very slowly on her. He started to kiss her neck, suck her lips, cheeks, breasts, pointed nipples and gradually shifted his mouth deeper. While she was undressing by his hands, his tongue was moving in her umbilicus, he had hurried to remove her dresses and threw them away. She said, "Someone may be seen us". Nikhila said' "I have early closed all of holes, don't be scared". Ahinsa allowed to suffer his desire as well as his needed. He was gained his summit soon, because he became crazy on over-lust of her. Then he didn't accept his first hesitation as a defeat, tried to kick-start again. In a very little time he got his re-erection, and this time he was able to ride the horse very skillfully. He didn't forget and didn't allow to leave any kind of her sensitive points at this second moment. He used her two times and she also highly satisfied, because she had spent for 14 months without an association of a male.

He got down the bed as a victorious warrior and offer her the thrown dress and helped her to getting dress. After the incident, Ahinsa didn't speak with him for about half an hour. Then Nikhila asked, "Do you hate me?" Ahinsa said, "No! Never, but please stay away from me for a while. I want to make my mind."

When Erandika returned to home, they usually had involved their usual routines, that often Nikhila was watching television and Ahinsa was feeding her child in her room. Apparently, as if there wasn't happened any strange event between them during the daytime.

Before long, Nikhila wanted to take a baby birth on his fatherhood from Ahinsa. Ahinsa didn't allow him to use her without a birth-controlling strategy. She asked, "Whenever if we will be caught to Erandika, what will you do?" Then Nikhila suddenly said, "Then let's be living together separately." Although, Nikhila doesn't expect to leave from Erandika as he had promised to her, he will never be left her on this bodily weakness about infertility of Erandika. Ahinsa also agreed to meet him secretly. Because it will be a severe conflict whenever with Priyanka and Erandika. Then Ahinsa was a very hard critical condition in that moment, because of missing her husband. Ahinsa promised to Nikhila, if her husband to be allowed to return with Nikhila's help, that means, Nikhila would like to help her to get return her husband, she will consider to let a baby to be conceived with her for Nikhila. Then Nikhila tried to trace about Priyanka. He wondered if Priyanka was in a prison in that country, to be paid the expenses to his returning. Because Priyanka didn't have committed with any criminal offence or infraction. Finally, after a hard perseverance, he was able to find the details about Priyanka and spent for his returning air tickets. Nikhila and Erandika had to apply a mortgage their jewelry for the expenses. Within a very short time duration, Priyanka returned. While he was returning, Ahinsa was very recently conceived from Nikhila. Then there wasn't born any confusion. That conceiving will be loaded on to her innocent husband's account. As their expectation, all of the events had been happened with Nikhila's desires. The secret confined among only Nikhila and Ahinsa. However, Priyanka came to home as a helpless person. He doesn't have any remains money. Otherwise' he was suffering from a disease with his backbone. Meanwhile, Ahinsa got ready for her second delivery. Nikhila was felt a very proud of her maturing baby in her, because he will be a father soon. He looked at her very eagerly and earnestly. She gave a birth of Nikhila's baby. A fantastic baby boy. She was loved the newly born baby more than the any other things of the world. But she never indicate it to the others, because she was in a small doubt as the baby looks like really Nikhila. She always thought about it, if they have hidden the past events between them, how they can hide the baby's external appearance, because whenever this child will be shown Nikhila's physical characteristics at the near future.

After for the relevant time duration, Priyanka was the father for both children. Although, they had taken more loans from Nikhila and Erandika, still couldn't reimburse even any coin. In addition, Ahinsa had taken more loans from Ahinsa's friends to support Priyanka's overseas job. Ahinsa extremely wanted to reimburse them. Priyanka didn't have any enthusiasm to repay the loans or earn for their usual expenses. Ahinsa tried to do many businesses, started to hardly emancipate from the loans. But also, she couldn't achieve her targets. Then she decided to take an overseas job. Because this country was in the verge of bankrupt. The monthly salaries of the local jobs were hardly ever enough to cover only the weekly expenses. The son of Nikhila and Ahinsa was entered to a primary school. His name was Dananja, was a very innocent, beautiful, intelligent and appreciated boy. He doesn't involve with quarrels with other peers looks like an innocent baby swan.

The stupid politicians and illegitimate government officials had devastated the economy of this country, by applying the misleading projects, money laundering, stealing the common taxes, taking high commissions for the foreign investments, and finally expressed their inability to pay the foreign loans. However, the politicians and the central banking top management also still highly boasting about their nakedness to be cheated the innocent people.

Brain-drain of the country, which means the educated, intelligent and professional experts of the country is being left this country for the foreign employments. The governors didn't allow to promote any kind of innovations and inventions of the young generation as they wanted to import all the vital or unnecessary stuffs. Because, they wanted to decrease the indigenous productions as the most local importers were the relations or directly family members of the illegitimate politicians. The ambassadors also who had appointed from the government were the non-educated and stupid companions or relations of those despicable politicians. The officials who have the ability to stealing or money laundering, still they are being committed these despicable thefts without any hesitation because receiving the powerful shelter of politicians, jurisprudents and lucrative shameless helpers. There were being appointed many numbers of bastard and non-educated wives of those shameless politicians as the chair persons on very important seats of economically very significant institutions of the country. As a result of these sleuthhound's useless decisions, the country was on the final verge of bankrupt. If, does anyone can't understand how to shift a country to proudly bankrupt condition, you can have more instructions the stupid governors of this miserable country.

Meanwhile, Ahinsa tried to leave the country as a housemaid. Her decision couldn't change to Nikhila, because of her owning with more loans. After about two years age of Nikihila's baby, that means second child of Ahinsa, she left from the country. The kids looked after by Nikhila and Erandika. Ahinsa gradually paid the earlier loans whatever she had taken by sending the money. Nikhila had to settle all of transactions as a moderator because Priyanka didn't have any kind of knowledge about banking transactions. She was able to settle the all kind of loans within five years. She had decided to work in abroad for at least seven years, because she didn't expect and believe about Priyanka's incoming. Meanwhile, Priyanka rarely worked if he has handed over any temporary task by someone. But he didn't take

the responsibility about the own child. That child had entered to the government school for his studies, but he also didn't care about learning. Then Ahinsa had sent money to them, buy a three-wheeler to be hired and earn. He, the child of Priyanka was a young man, rather a mischievous and playful.
The boy named **"Dananja",** who adopted with Nikhila and Erandika was a well-mannered student with all kind of skills with education and sports. One day, he was committed in an accident during playing in his school. He had fell down from a staircase as one of his friends had pulled him to down. It was not extremely purposed to injure him, but also it had been occurred. Then his skull had wounded seriously.

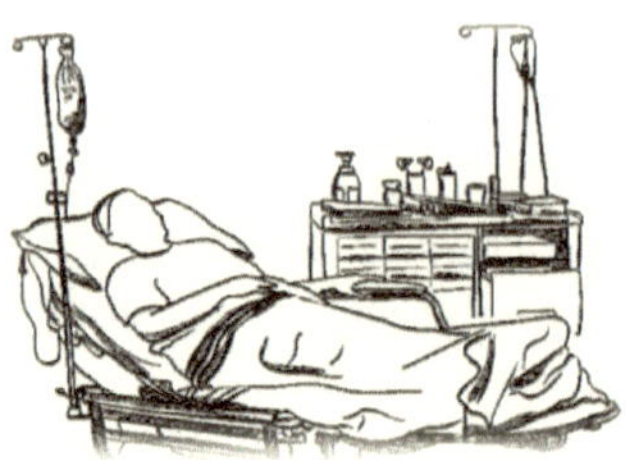

The boy was hospitalized. He was rather a complicated position, and had to blood transfusion soon. But the relevant blood group was not found the blood bank of the hospital at that moment, wanted to blood donor with consanguinity. Then, the doctor informed to Nikhila and Erandika to suddenly donate his father's blood, for the child. Then Erandika called to Priyanka. He urgently came to the hospital and committed for the blood testing and unfortunately, failed his blood group. Then Nikhila had to submit his blood sample for testing as Erandika's severe request. "Sometimes, your blood group might be supposedly matched with the son's blood group, it will be the fortune of the son". Then Nikhila couldn't neglect her request, because the boy was in a severe critical condition. After the result of blood testing, Nikhila's blood group was really matched with Dananja's blood group. Erandika was approached in an impatient doubtful mind, but didn't ask anything from Nikhila because the boy in a hard condition. Priyanka also disappointedly left the hospital and thought more about Ahinsa.
Within a few days, Dananja was able to discharge from the hospital, gradually he was cured completely. Dananja usually addressed Nikhila called, "Uncle" and Erandika was called, "Aunt". As usually Dananja started go to school. One Sunday, Nikhila and Erandika were at home, because that was a holy day although Dananja had to leave the home for his tuition class. After that blood transfusion, they didn't speak more if unless there wasn't in an essential need. Specially, Nikhila omitted her eyes. Erandika was impatiently looking for a suitable time to blast that hidden bomb, Erandika Said, "Don't try to further cheat me, tell me the truth! Nikhila, look at me, who is the father of Dananja!" "What are you talking Erandhika, do you want to scatter our family life, by arousing an unnecessary past background?" said Nikhila. He didn't have any need to leave the home at the moment, but he got ready and left soon.
He came to a nearest restaurant and selected a deserted table. He ordered a hot drink. While sipping it, he got a call to Ahinsa. He explained the current problem that he had faced with her. She also early had known about the problem, because

Priyanka had called her and had harshly scolded her about her past behavior. But she didn't have accepted the accusation. Then Priyanka had said with her, that he wanted to make a DNA test with Dananja. Ahinsa had said to him, "If you will do so, I will never come back to mother land. If you want to ever leave me, go and get tested on any kind of matter, I will never send any money to you!" Therefore, Priyanka had to hesitate, because he doesn't like to deprive the money that Ahinsa is being sent to him. But he had asked Ahinsa, "I was detained abroad only one and half years, although you couldn't keep my dignity for our child, I can't understand how you would behave in the present time at the overseas! Then I will never belive you as a reliable wife." Then Priyanka's questing will be stopped. But Erandika won't give up this matter easily and lightly. She will never leave the question when she quested the true. "Now, where are you?" asked Ahinsa. Nikhila explained the event that why did he leave the home and where was he in that moment." "Go home soon, don't leave your wife, she is an innocent and now may be in an unaffordable sorrow. You should be extremely more patient and stay calm whatever she will tell you, because we are not perfect in this time, we have done an uncorrectable mistake at the past. We should understand about it. Now you should have a self-confidence to solve the problem as I only wanted to make fulfil your request of your own baby in my womb, then Nikhila, please, please just now go home and try to console your wife, and remember, you must never allow her to conduct a DNA test of Dananja. And you also extremely will have to careful for keep off from a DNA test", Ahinsa harshly advised me.

Nikhila finished his ordered stuff and paid the bill soon. He wanted to stay away from the home until Dananja returned home. While he was in the home, Erandika won't make any question about the trouble, and the time rotating is the best remedy for such these questions. Then Nikhila made his mind to be faced any kind of a future condition with Erandika.

Nikhila waited for a while when Dananja leave from his tuition class and reached to the home with him. Then Erandika didn't speak even any word with Nikhila for few days. But one night, Dananja had slept. Erandika wanted to arouse the problem again. Erandika said, "I don't mind if you have selected any other woman for to get conceived your child! But why did you select Ahinsa for it, she is my own brother's wife." "Even if I wanted to make my own child, if my wife had ever failed for it, what is the wrong of that decision I had taken to get my own child from another suitable woman?" Nikhila argued with his mind. "However, Dananja is my own child. Why can't Erandika accept this truth?" Nikhila thought. "Why don't you reply for my question, tell me, who is the father of Dananja? Erandika was in a harsh fury. Nikhila got his anger and he frantically shouted, "I told once you! Don't ask again and again on the same question, if you want to solve the problem, you should take a decision whether you accept Dananja is our own son or not. Because we didn't have any kind of question about his fatherhood before his accident". He took his pillow and other stuff and get off the room. He didn't have a sleepy, because He had to fight with my mind to be taken a decision. Nikhila thought further. "I should leave this home for a few days, unless I should be left my life!

Next Sunday also Erandika asked the same question. The time was about 9.30 a.m. "Tell me the truth, if Dananja was not a son of Priyanka, if Ahinsa accommodated in this home for one and half years, if both of you were here alone in some days without me, tell me Nikhila, wouldn't you be the real father of Nikhila?" Erandika asked. "Ask it with Ahinsa!" Nikhila shouted and continued, "She may know, the real father of Dananja?" "Okay, let's go to a DNA test, why do you omit my request, if you do not have involved in any sexy event with Ahinsa, you must have an encouragement for such a test", Erandika firmly said. Then usually Nikhila leaves the home soon. While he is leaving the home, Erandika said, "You will have to leave the home ever, if you will be failed to give me a direct answer for my question." I will never reply for your question, even if I would be died." Nikhila said and left the home. Usually, he selected the restaurant table and ordered the drinks. While he is drinking, he took a call to Ahinsa and said the condition. "I love my child Ahinsa! I love our child Ahinsa, but I can't tolerate those innuendoes of Erandika, I feel like to suicide myself. But I want to ask the word dad or father from my son's mouth, even only once a time during my life time" Ahinsa replied, "Don't be a fool Nikhila, if you love me, if you love your child, if you love our child, please be calm and make your mind to be faced the truth". "I am so sorry Ahinsa, I will try to hide my fatherhood ever from Dananja, I will do so, yes, I promise you, during my lifetime, I will never reveal that secret!" He returned to home at 10.30 pm. and didn't speak any word with anyone. He had highly intoxicated and couldn't control himself. Dananja was sleeping in his room and Erandika was in the living room of foyer by watching TV. He entered the bath room and after having a wash, directly went to the bed. "Don't you take dinner?" Erandika asked. But, by the time Nikhila had slept.

The next day, in the morning, Erandika and Dananja usually were getting ready to leave the home. Nikhila was still sleeping. Erandika said to Dananja, "Get awake your uncle to ready to leave for the work". Dananja tried to do so, but also Nikhila didn't answer. Nikhila had died on the bed! Then, Dananja identified the condition, "Aunt, Aunt! Uncle doesn't speak!" They found a letter had written by Nikhila.

Dear Erandika,

I do accept my fault. I never thought to write my final word like this. But please never ask that question repeatedly. I request you to please don't insult to Ahinsa. I will never be answered for your last question. I love you ever! Be a real poster mother to Dananja. I have been arranged my all benefits of insurance policy for you and to Dananja. Forget me ever.

Nikhila.

The funeral of Nikhila was conducted calmly. The postmortem had revealed, Nikhila had used more and high dosage of anesthetic with liquor. Erandika or Priyanka didn't inform to Ahinsa about Nikhila's dead. But Dananja had informed her. Ahinsa had said with Dananja, "I will never come to my country again."

The time passed gradually. Erandika started to involve her official duties. Dananja went to school. Priyanka frequently came to their home and helped to ease their workload. After three weeks of Nikhila's funeral, one night, about 10.30 pm, a stranger tapped on the front door. Erandika was sleeping in her room. Dananja was studying in his room. Tapping of the door heard a few times. Dananja came out from his room and stepped at the front door and asked, "Who you are?" No one answered. He detained at the door for a few minutes. But didn't receive an answer. Then he returned his room. He thought that tapping sound might be an illusion of his mind. But he had talked about it with Erandika in the next morning.

At the same time of the next night, that tapping sound emerged. Dananja went to the front door and usually asked, "What is the matter, what do you want?" But there wasn't an answer. Dananja didn't inform about the second incident with Erandika because she might be scared. The third day also emerged the same condition at the same time. Dananja didn't open the door but asked, "Tell me, who you are, what do you want, unless I would have call to the police!"

"My dear son, Dananja! I want to see your face even a once time! I love you my son", said the stranger. Dananja thought, Priyanka had come at this moment within intoxicated. But the voice of the stranger was familiar him. But he couldn't understand whose voice is that. It was rather same with Nikhila. However, he opened the door. But he couldn't see anyone at the door. Then he closed the door, locked it properly and took the bed of his room. Dananja bothered about half an hour to be identified the strange familiar voice. How Nikhila can speak with him, as he had died recently. Nikhila was being highly loved to Dananja. Dananja often remembered, he had a few times requested by Nikhila, "Dear son, don't address me as uncle, I would like to ask from you addressing me father or dad!" Then Dananja took a decision to fearlessly face this stranger. Because he was a teenager, didn't have any hesitation to face the adventurous or scary events. The next day also emerged that tapping sound at the same time and Dananja directly opened the door! Dananja surprised and scared because Nikhila was there in front of the door. Dananja really identified, he was Nikhila. When Nikhila is living, Dananja was taught by him to don't make any fear to haunts or ghosts because if they will appear in front of you, they would expect something like help or reveal some secret with you. Dananja had read more books, magazines and articles about haunts and ghosts as Nikhila preferred to read them. Then Dananja made his self-confidence to speak with this inhuman soul. "Tell me uncle, what you want?" he asked. "I will never come to be a burden with you hereafter, please address me only once a time, "Dad or father" because I am your real father!" Dananja had been implied about this matter early while living Nikhila. Then Dananja said, "Dad, I love you ever!" Nikhila hugged him but there wasn't an animate body. Then Nikhila said, "I love you too, don't tell this secret with any one, I will never be appear in front of you and in front of this world!" Danuja started to cry in Nikhila's arms. They shared the affection of father between an own son, but no more time. Nikhila suddenly disappeared.

Ahinsa didn't return to her native country. She sent an adequate amount of money to Dananja, Priyanka and elder son of Ahinsa who was lived with his father of Priyanka. After about five years of Nikhila's death, Erandika got married with an affluence, divorced middle aged man who was working in the same office with her. He didn't expect the kids from Erandika. Priyanka was addicted to liquor and didn't have an enthusiasm to find a sex life. Ahinsa had ever loved to Nikhila. She might not have intended to involve to settle with Priyanka if she had early identified his addiction for liquor. However, Nikhila shouldn't have selected that innocent woman, Ahinsa for succeed his selfishness and unethical necessity about an own baby or quench his beastly lust.

I didn't give up my quest on haunts and ghosts. When I was further exploring that events, I found very fabulous stories about them. One day I went to be participated a funeral of my relative adult person. I spent for a few hours in that home, because the coffin was deposited in the foyer of the relevant home for tribute the body because the relatives, friends, neighbors and acquaintances who early associated with the deceased person, before his demise have been gathering to the funeral. The time was about 1.30 pm, the traditional funeral customs had been organized at 5.00 pm. Then I had to spend for about three hours in the place. While I was sitting on a chair in a shelter of a tree in that front yard, one of my old friends came at me. I couldn't recognize him initially because he worn a mask as it was the outbreak period of Covid pandemic. Then he removed the mask in front of me to see his face. I suddenly recognized him, **Mr. Wijith Kulasooriya**, as he was one of old friends of mine. We had been working in a same industry for few years in eastern province of the country. Then we started to chat about the things in various interesting past events that were occurred among us. I was suffering from a harsh thirsty on exploring about the haunts and ghosts, then I dragged the subject. He also was a severe interesting about them and he started to narrate a wonderful ghosting story what he had experienced early.

After having his retirement of the job, he had been manipulated his mind to be found a suitable place for his residence. At the time, he had a significant amount of money because he had released his pension fund and had saved some money during his working period. His wife also had been engaged into a private company as an accountant, then they had more money. Then they wanted to buy a spacious land with a coconut cultivation. He had travelled and searched such a land from the newspaper advertisements. Finally they could purchase a fantastic land. As he explained the event on his own words, "There was a large abandoned and deserted mansion amidst the land. The land was surrounded with a huge wall as that couldn't see out of the land or in side of the land. The fundamental owner of the land was a person who owned into the old aristocracy of the country. I decided to completely modify that mansion and reinforce the building for our residency. We started to rehabilitate it by manipulating some workers. While the maintenances are continuing, some workers had been leaving the workplace. I had to frequently recruit the workers. The workers were well-paid by me and provided the meals for them. They had to prepare the meals in the mansion where we have early temporary built hut. They were provided day and night accommodation in the mansion during the working period. They were not familiar for the region because they had come to my work from the various regions of the country. I was inquisitively searched the reasons for their leaving. One of masons who was appointed as the head bass, informed me a strange matter that has been occurring at the night time in this mansion. Because, I didn't stay in the mansion at night time as we have decided to stay away from the mansion until finishing the repairs. We wanted to reside in it after converting it as a very innovative place. Then we detained in a nearby rented home until completely finishing the maintaining works. I was able to know, there were strange and perilous sounds at night time in the mansion. I never believed the haunts and ghosts. However, we were able to conclude the maintenances within four months. My wife suggest to be conducted a reputed religious observance before our residing in the mansion. I have hidden that rumor about the strange sounds of the mansion because the ladies make scare to stay with haunts. I very willingly agreed to that suggestion. We organized a religious observance as well as we could. We went to the nearest temple and met the monk. Typically, I didn't respect the monks as they were being played double games by cheating the innocent people in the country. But, unexpectedly the chief monk of this temple was a very virtuous and was a highly educated, honorable clergy. We appointed a suitable date and conducted a religious observant correctly.

We resided in that fresh mansion. My son and daughter also were with us and happily started the new life. Within a week, I was able to hear the strange sounds at the night time as said that chief mason. I didn't care about the sounds and got slept. I regularly could hear the sounds at the night like walking a person, arouse the utensils of the kitchen. Then I wanted to search the kitchen, and I suddenly entered to the kitchen. The light was lighting, the refrigerator had opened. The gas cooker had been burning. But nothing was there anyone. I closed the refrigerator, turned off the gas cooker and switched off the light. Then suddenly that perilous sound emerged in front of the main door. I hastily came at the door. Then, anyone tapped on the door. My hair was erected, heart rapidly beaten. I took a deep breath and thought a moment. Then the tapping was emerged again and someone called me, "**Mr. Kulasooriya**, don't fear, please open the door, I have to tell you something and I want to give you a gift!" said the stranger. "Please come at a day time, check the time now please." I said angrily. The stranger said, "I can't appear at the day time." Then I made my mind and took an iron bar with my right hand, to be dared any kind of terrible opportunity, switched on the lights of veranda and slowly opened the door!" There was a man who worn a cassock! But there isn't his head, only the black hollow! Indeed, there wasn't a head with his body. My blood was warmed. Actually I was scared. But I came soon into my presence, and looked at his head. “Don’t worry about my head, it is with my hands on a tray”, he said. I suddenly looked at the tray. I couldn’t believe it. There was a skull on a tray with him. I want to tell you something, Please, please, listen to me!” I amazed and looked at him. He said, “I am professor, **Edverd Hussim**. I was the first owner of this mansion. I made this mansion in 1812, please take this skull and bury it with tributes as your religious manners. I tried to do this with previous owners who resided early of this mansion. But they frightened me and left the mansion. You will find the fortune of your whole family life everlastingly, when you properly bury this skull in front that huge teak tree really oriented to eastern side at nine feet from the root of the tree. My treasure is there, please promise me. You can find more details about me when you bury this skull as my instructions!” I promised him and said, “I don’t need your properties, but I promise you to highly achieve your request tomorrow, as well as my ability.” I said. Then he disappeared suddenly. I searched the skull but it also had disappeared. Then I closed the door and turned to in side of the home. Fabulously, that skull was there on the stool that I established to keep the newspapers. I suddenly closed it with a clear kerchief and kept the stool invisibly.

Next morning, I immediately called a family discussion and described the incident with my all family members. Because my son and daughter were the adolescent students and were comprehensive ages.

Then I quickly left the home to meet the monk of the temple. I met the chief monk who conducted the religious observances of my residing moment of this mansion. Then the monk said with me, “That mansion was initially had owned to a foreign professor who resided in this country to be explored the Buddhist Philosophy and the ancient culture in 1811.” I wanted to know more details about that professor, but the monk didn’t have any idea about him. The monk was not born at the time, he had heard the story from his parents when he was a very young man, before he enter to priesthood. I invited the monk to be conducted the customary and traditional religious observances without omitting any kind of cults. I got a list of stuff for the funeral of the skull. While I was returning, I went to buy the sacrificial items that had written on the list. In the evening, at about 4.00 pm, the monk came to our mansion with an assistant and prepared the funeral. I cared to do it very well-prepared manner as I had promised to successfully do it without having any shortage. I dug a suitable pit with my son for the skull where the real place that ghost said. Before the monk’s arrival I had arrange to dig a pit for the skull. While we were digging it, we were able to find a small curved precious box had buried the appointed place. My son tried to open it by removing the protective cover, although I prevented to opening it because the skull is still not respectfully buried. Then the box was hidden by us and I told to my son, do not touch it or do not reveal with anyone about the hidden box.

After concluding the monk's religious customs, we all together, that means all of our family members had participated the funeral, prayed to charge a wholesome emancipation with Mr. Edverd Hussim. The skull was respectfully deposited in a box and took it in front of the said huge teak tree.

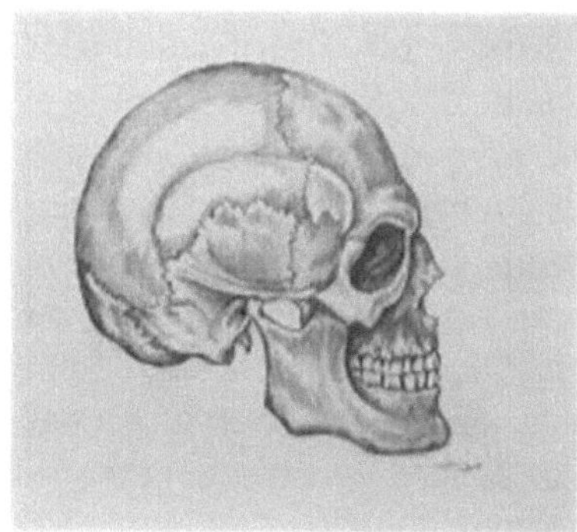

The monk and assistant left the mansion with my favorable donation, what I offered for their dedication in the matter. We took out that hidden small box and carefully opened it. There was a letter.

For the attention those who are allowed to find this letter.

I am Edverd Hussim a professor who came to this country to be explored the Philosophy of Buddhism and ancient religion cults. I built this mansion for my residence by expecting to be lived in this country with my wife and children. Initially I came alone to here with the prior permission of my country's government. Because, this country is a colony of my motherland. I was imprisoned in a room of my own house by some indigenous people who have employed by me in this mansion as my servants. Their intension would be robbed my properties. But also, I had hidden them early under the foyer of my mansion. If I was committed to be killed me by these people, please take my hoard and make my funeral according with the customs of Buddhist philosophy. After that, the hoard should divided as follows.

For religious monasteries - 10%.
For helpless people - 10%
For infirmaries - 10%
You will be able to take the rest of hoard freely.

Edverd Hussim. 22.08.1816

We could find a rectangular mark amidst the foyer of the mansion. At the night time, we dug the place. About in two feet deeply, we found a wooden box. We opened it and were able to find some very highly precious gems and some of highly valuable jewelries.

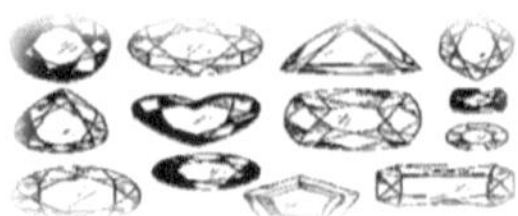

We deeply thanked to Mr.Edverd in a religious manner and prayed to rest in peace of his soul. Then he didn't appear after the event.

But I drastically wanted to find how Mr. Edverd died." We had to stop our discussion as the funeral of my relation is going to be started. Then I took his phone number. We were unable to chat again, because we had to leave the place soon after the funeral. We left the place having being completed the funeral.

Before long, I had a call and made an appointment with Mr. Wijith. He invited me to his home. I really attended his home at the punctual time that we have appointed over the phone. While I was attending there, he was watching the television, and he cordially welcomed me.

He had arranged a nice liquor party for me. When we tasted, I saw his home arrangements. Of course it was not a simple home, apparently it was a real mansion and he lived in it with his family as a baron. He used a luxurious vehicle.

He started to speak about the subject where we have stopped at that funeral. First of all, he had divided the hoard as the manner of the letter. The rest of them, he had bought a luxurious vehicle and some other allotments with a few farms. Then he doesn't involve in any employment as he had a sufficient income. He usually started with a glass of liquor with his hand, "I wanted to investigate about Professor Edverd and how he had died. Especially I wanted to know, had he suffered from our indigenous barbarian people.

There was a very poor family nearby this mansion, that householder, called by the villagers as "Moodiya" was appointed by Edverd as a watcher in the land. There were more acres in the land with coconut cultivation. Then there were another vacancy for a watcher. Because Edverd had identified the people who are being lived in this country since at the past were drastically thieves. If they have an opportunity, they would actually ready to steal their mothers' dresses. Edverd was informed by Moodiya to find a suitable person to be filled the vacancy. Moodiya wanted to appoint one of his brothers for the vacancy. As his request, Edverd had selected the person. The brothers were very cunning people who have ascended as offspring of very immoral and stupid generation. There was a house hold servant in the mansion in addition to that watchers. That two siblings had noticed, there is an only person in the mansion as the owner. Then they planned to kill him and get the possession of the mansion and Edverd's properties. They had manipulated the household servant to collect the poison with Edverd's meals. The household servant had ignored the proposal once. Then that siblings had promised him to separate a part of the properties. Even unwillingly he also had agreed for that sinful proposal.

The cunning siblings had planned to kill the servant after succeeding their first achievement. The servant was provided a kind of severe poisonous liquid by the siblings. Before long, the servant gave the poison to Edverd, but also he didn't die at once. While Edverd was gradually in a serious position and struggling to survive his life on a very dangerous and hard unaffordable painful condition, those siblings had immediately come to the mansion. They had cruelly cut and separated Edverd's neck.

Having concluded the inhuman homicide, the torso, the trunk without the head inserted into a sack. The head inserted into another sack. Siblings decided to remove that two sacks into a nearby deep and steep river. More cannibal crocodiles were in the river. They impatiently were looking for the darkness to bring out the sacks. They decided to bring them separately, because in case anyone could make doubt of them if the sacks were carrying at once.

About 7.30 pm, the sacks were brought to out of the mansion and observantly brought them at the nearby river side.

While they carrying them, they could see two neighbors were coming on the way. A sack with the head of Edverd was invisibly hidden by siblings under a grown bush and the sack with torso dragged hurriedly onto the river bank and pulled it into the river. After moving the neighbors on their way, they came to take the hidden sack. But it had disappeared because it would be dragged by an animal. They tried to find it, but also couldn't find. Then they gave up the purpose of finding the head of Edverd. They returned to the mansion and cleaned the place where the crime was committed. The siblings advised and instructed the partner in crime the servant who applied the poison with Edverd's meals about the future plan. The siblings returned their homes that had been provided them by Edverd to be lived during their tenure. As if the innocent people, they came to the mansion in the next morning and pretended a severe sorrowful performance.

Within about three weeks, the colonial governors involved to observe the disappearance of Professor Edverd, but they couldn't find any kind of evidence. The servant hide the details and didn't reveal anything on the impact of the barbarian siblings. Before long, the servant had committed to an unexpected demise in the mansion on an unknown reason. He had revealed with the siblings before his death,

about unidentified haunting events in the mansion. The servant had drastically frightened. The siblings were also committed such the unanticipated events and had died within two weeks after the demise of the servant. There was a rumor about a corpse with a skull is being haunted in the mansion."
I wanted to know, how Mr.Kulasooriya found the further details about that haunting story without being lived any kind of eye witnesses or other kind of witnesses, because that incident had been occurred on 200 years ago. Mr. Kulasooriya said, "That is the most important question in this event. I also earnestly wanted to reveal the enigma of murder of professor Edverd. I thought, how I should commence the mission for this quest. Finally, I decided to meet the monk who had involved that religious observances for the skull of Edverd. I went to the temple and spoke with the monk. Initially he didn't reveal anything about the families of that homicidal siblings. I persuaded to the monk, that incident had happened in approximately nearby 1816. This is the year of 2022. Then there are only 206 years difference. Then can you count that, at least only 3 historical generations could pass their life time in the duration. The murders could possessed into past fourth previous generation. Then I believed, if the monk was a person who had born in this village, he would have known the generations of that servant and the murders who had worked in this property. I early had launched an investigation to find about the families who are living around this coconut land. There are about 15 houses and 15 families are currently living to verging border of this land. They had forcibly invaded the bordering allotments of this huge land. I have studied the main plan in the land register, although, there isn't any noticeable evidence to legally possessing that invaded land allotments of that currently residents. But also, they had got prepared the deeds for those lands by having a huge shelter of a former influential politician. Then I found the details further, if one of that murders had been born nearly at 1760 and had been lived at least 70 years, he would die on 1830, and his offspring generation also lived for 70 years, they would die around 1900, if their generation also lived for 70 years, they would die 1970. If a person had born in around 1970, they would be lived currently, then we can find their history. I could reveal the said families had generated only four fatherhoods initially in the duration of 1830 to 1900s. That means, there were only four houses around this land by the past murderous sibling's generation from 1760 to 1830. Their offspring were lived 1830 to 1900 with newly made three houses. Their offspring had built newly five houses in 1900 to 1970. The current generation had built only three new houses including the previous houses had been modified. There was a huge home which possessed to that influential politician who had been elected as the president of this country. The said president with his family was famed and had been gained a victorious achievements for money laundering, thefts, exploiting the innocent people, killing the opposite journalists and misusing the government taxes by collaborating with his barbarian companions. There is a rumor among the people in this country, that politician also was an offspring of one of the murderous siblings.

We had to participate with the alms giving ceremony of Prishan's grandmother. We gathered to Prishan's home. There was a tradition with the beliefs of religion, which the soul of deceased person will be made with emancipation at his next rebirth by alms giving to the monks. After seven days of the death of that person, the said alms giving ceremony should have been conducted. Then, the participants of the funeral were invited by those residents of the home where the dead person was being lived in his or her lifetime. The staff of our institute had also called for that charitable purpose. We participated the event and all of us helped the ceremony as we had gone there very early. We had to help them to the decorations, made the canopies, sweep and clean the yard. Typically, helping such events were a usual function of the friends. We had brought some bottles of liquor to be used after the ceremony, especially we wanted to further continue Nirasha's story. Having conducted the all-ceremonial customs, we helped to rearrange the furniture, because early we had made spacious dining place to the monks by removing the furniture of their living room. Having completed the workload, the monks left the home. We gathered for the discussion. Dinuja and I arranged the table with the bottles, and after chatting about the success of the alms giving ceremony, I had to make reminder where we had concluded the story. We sat the same place with the stuff for chatting where we settled last week. Without being wasted out our time, I got down into the capital topic what I had to know.

Prishan restarted, "The most considerable and unique incident had been reported after a year in time of that early death of kiththa, at the same place. The dead body of Podde had been found by the police around the bridge on the river bank, as Prishan says, where the place I met that girl. As he says, that body also had been defaced and had extremely covered significant evidence. When the investigation employed could have been found, there had been written the name of the murderer, "Nirasha" on the floor as near as possible to the corpse. How could Nirasha's name been written near the body of Podde?

According to the Podde's mother had expressed, since long ago, Podde had started an affair with a married woman. Her husband had abandoned her as her harlotry. Then Podde was a rakish and reckless young man, didn't consider about the future, and was a short-sighted man. His mother had advised for few times to Podde, to be kept off and stay away from that prostitute. He didn't have accepted the mother's instructions. Then at the night times, he usually had entered to that woman's home. He had spent all of his earnings for that prostitute woman. Gradually, Podde had omit his own responsibility for his innocent mother. Podde's father had died early by falling on a coconut tree when he tried to stealthily pluck the nuts from another's land without being taken the permission. Then, Podde and his mother had been lived hardly. Then Podde's mother maintained a little cattle farm for their existence. Podde didn't have an encouragement to hardworking. He wanted to earn a lot of money without working. Because his mother had helped him while he was attending to the school, by bringing his all stuff with her to the school, washing his clothes and podde had become an idle, lazy, vagabond useless man. His mother didn't have taught him to be a responsible citizen. The government school teachers are also not considering about this condition, always applying only parents help for any kind of workload without being deploying the students' capability. Then he decided to work with Tiran because Podde was paid a significant payment by Tiran for engaging his under handed businesses such as dealing with drug sellers, collecting ransoms from the persons who gained the facilities of his father, ransoms from the illegally appointed or promoted officials in the government institutes. They monthly gathered ransoms even the labors who appointed by them in to the governmental hospitals as attendants. Are there any other shameless company of politicians and sons in the world like the people in this country????

The police had decided that name was "Nirasha" where had been written near by the deceased person at his dying moment. This was not an extreme robbery, because there was a purse with some less money, the identity card, and the driving license of the dead man. The registered motorcycle owned by Tiran had been ridden by Podde that night also was there near the bridge. That also happened under the supervision of a full moon.

Podde's casual woman also had given a statement to the police. According to that statement, Podde had come to her home at about 10.30 pm, and had left her home about 11.30 pm by the motor cycle. He also had selected the short cut were laid on the perilous bridge. But anyone doesn't believe, Podde would never be willingly got down the river or river bank, because the people had known there were cannibal crocodiles in the river. Then was there any hidden enigma with the bridge?

"But the police were unable to find any clue. We, the members of our family were questioned by the police, according to the name mentioned on the floor", said Prishan and filled the glass. The inquiry file of the corpse of Podde also had hidden by the police under the deepest corner of the cupboard with the other hidden files.

By considering all the events, our grandmother suspected and deeply believed that the soul of Nirasha was being revenged by killing the partners who had been involved as the accomplice with Tiran's stupid and mischievous things. We also had to believe it. But we still adhere and believe that all criminals will be definitely punished by her as soon as possible. Prishan wanted to go away for a moment. Then he stopped his narration. He came back soon with a file of papers and restarted.

Nirasha's parents had a severe necessity to know what had happened to Nirasha. Then Nirasha's mother who was unaffordable grieved and was looking impatiently to be known what had happened to Nirasha, if Nirasha was suffered a sorrowful event by any criminals and legally punish the criminals who committed this crime and frequently wished to know about her disappearance and punish the offenders. She sacrificed for succeed her intention. She wanted to know if, whether Nirasha appeared on the bridge and killed that people. Nirasha's mother very tightly believed the religion, and lived in accordance with traditional cults. One day she took some flowers, incense sticks, oil lamp and frankincense. She went with them near the said bridge. She prepared them on a flat stone in a sacrificing manner and started to pray. She had done it for three days with a harshly venerated emotion. The last day, suddenly had appeared the image of Nirasha, had worn her favorite

and calm dressing and had said, "My dear mother! Don't worry about me. I will punish the criminals. Please stay away from this bridge! I will have been gained my emancipation after punishing them. Please don't regret about me, I will definitely rebirth in a well-being society according to my imaginative power. Otherwise, you don't regret me about how a pain would I was suffered at my dying moment by those beasts, no mother, I didn't have suffered at least stinging me a mosquoto! Because I was left my mind from my body before my dying moment, they could push under this bridge only my mindless, and visualize body, now also here is appearing only my astral-body!" And she disappeared soon. Then Nirasha's family believed that appearance of Nirasha on the bridge. Then I clearly understood, that is the reason why Nirasha's mother tried to prevent me to select the shortcut laid on the bridge in that night when I was returned after dropping Prishan.
I wanted to find more details about astral-body of a person. I started a special research for finding about it.

The astral body is an ultra-fine body that means, as delicate or precise as to be difficult to analyze be kept forward as a basis of imaginative energy of a psychological power in a human mind. That special power can be consisted with a person who had highly practiced with controlling the own concentration by meditating in a proper manner with dedicating the soul power. In some religious philosophies of the world had described in a well-mannered way how to improve a mind of a person, and why should we gain a harmless life or why should we leave from the sinful lifestyle. Because if we have a re-birth of after death, we will have to carry only that sinful mind because we will never be able to carry with us any kind of sources to our grave and beyond in additional far. But also, if we have empowered our mind by omitting the sinful concepts such as desire, envious, revenge, animosity, greed, covetousness and illimitable lust, we will be able to send our astral mind into a great heaven. Then, our life style should have been early selected the most suitable asceticism that omitting the sinful actions. The middle way, that means very justifiable way is the most suitable to reach to the enlightenment.

The concept of this astral-body is defined in common worldwide religious philosophies of the afterlife in which the soul's departure or "ascent" is described as out of body experience, that the spiritual explorer omits the physical body and travels in his ultra-fine body that means dream body or astral body into his early intended purpose. Therefore, power of disappearance also related in this concept, but the astral body is able to appear in other place but also the real body is existing in an unconscious condition at the place he leave the body. The phenomenon of apparitional experience is also related with this concept. Then we can understand, the body and the mind are collaborated and made a creature, but also these are not a same unit. The astral body is sometimes defined, it can be appeared as an aural bangle, as any kind of animate figure or untouchable picture. Then anyone wouldn't been able to say, an astral body of some creature is should have appeared as certain visual body. Because according to his or her mighty of imaginative power, can be changed the visual figure time to time.

Tiran and his father had started to gain their political power and started a canvassing campaign for the election, because there had been arranged to conduct an election for elect the parliament members. Already that time duration, Tiran's father was a chairman of provincial council of the area. The next step of such a politician was the ambition to be a member of parliament. Then they laboriously worked for achieve their targets. Tiran was the chief organizer of the campaign. The opposite competitor was an educated person who had been engaged with University Grants commission. Then Nirasha's father also had supported the opposite competitor of Tiran's father. Tiran's party members and supporters were engaged with aggressive behavioral conductions, because they were the influential with power. But also, nothing had done for the people, always only had unjustifiably collected the own property by committing with money laundering, illegally capturing the lands, getting the bribes and commissions from the contractors. They had a liquor shop, a fuel shed and a stone quarry. All of these properties had been taken by them by using their unjustifiable money. Briefly, Tiran's father was an immoral dictator.
Tiran also followed his father's barbarian path. On his non-educated background, he had used to misuse his father's political power. However, at the next election, this immoral politician and his son will have been defeated by the opposition. The opposition candidate had gained a high prestige among the people. The people had started to criticize them. The officials of police and other government departments had decided to help the opposition. Only some immoral and lucrative officials were to help the current government, but they have already had stepped back because the people's wave was been powered to the opposition.

Although, Tiran was usually existing his playfulness life. There was an appointed secretary in his father's office called **Tanya.** Tanya was working in that office for a few months on temporary basis. Typically, that the young girls are being recruited such that politician's office duties on that casual basis because the tenure of that politician would be concluded at the next election as he might be failed to recollect the adequate quantity of votes on his ill-mannered working background and weaknesses of governing. Tanya was rather an attractive, beautiful and sexy figured young girl. Tiran's enthusiasm had been committed for her. He frequently hovered around her and looked at her with inviting and lusty eyes. Tanya was a poor girl who was expecting a permanent job by his father's help. Tiran planned to involve with her to temporary indulgence. He trended to cheat her by promising to appoint her in a government office for a permanent job. Then Tanya believed him. Tiran proposed her to face for an interview for such an employment. Tiran gave her an address, date and a proper time to be participated for an interview. Tanya reached the place at the punctual time with one of her friends. Her partner, that means the girl who gathered with Tanya, was police officer because Tanya's boyfriend has collected her to participate for the interview as a proctor of Tanya. That building was a large private home, looks like a five stars hotel. But Tanya didn't have a scary emotion because she had a thoughtful boyfriend and he had known about Tiran. That boyfriend also went with her but didn't appear with them, although chased them as a pursuer. He invisibly followed them. Then she knew if there will be approached any wickedness event by Tiran, her boyfriend will be appeared soon. That boyfriend was working in the police department, he early had guest definitely

Tiran will try to trap on his girlfriend, because Tanya had early revealed those cupid activities of Tiran whatever had done on her. Then her boyfriend had arranged an urgent scheme by discussing with his department head, if there will be risen any kind of wicked event to be activated immediately. He had used a mobile button phone as the pones had initially introduced into the country.

There was a job interviewing center in that home. The girls who faced to the interviews can be faced the interview and offered a drink with powdered sleeping tablets. After that drink, the girls were carried the inside rooms and the early settled buyers were waiting there for the selected girl. The boys also had taken to the interview but they had sent back because the boys' interviews were fake action. But the organizers had strategically led them to another floor. Tiran was impatiently waiting in a room with highly dreaming about Tanya. Tanya's boyfriend also entered to the hotel as a candidate, but the males were not provided a same drink. But also, he didn't drink their beverage, but sipped for pretended only, spying about Tanya. Tanya was also pretended as drinking the offered beverage and showed drowsiness and taken her into a room. Suddenly His boyfriend took a call to his station and within ten minutes that hotel was surrounded by the police. Because the police officials had previously received more anonymous complains from the victims about this place. They wanted to trap the criminals with non-breakable evidence. Tiran's father also possesses the shares due some politicians were the shareholders of this job interviewing center due to that illegal whore house was being conducted by the influential group of businessmen of the area. Tanya was taken in to a room by some working girls. Tiran was in the room with having liquor and cannabis smoke. Tanya was laid on the bed because she pretended as sleeping. The other police woman officer who came with Tanya also was taken to another room. She also pretended as drowsy. Tanya was halfway undressed by Tiran. Her blouse buttons were detached. Her bra was shifted from her beautiful fair breasts. Tiran kissed her neck, breasts and his right hand was pushing out her skirt. Her fantastic thighs were appeared as heaven's gate.

Tiran impatiently kissed her panties for three minutes and tried to undress her. Suddenly the police team snapped into the room. They arrested Tiran. A few influential people had been arrested by the police. The offenders were lodged in to the court and were imprisoned. The accused persons were able to release on bails. They had to keep a sum of considerable amount of money be lodged to guarantee their appearance in court.

Tiran never thought and never known that who had made that trap for him. However, Tanya didn't go to her work into their office. But also, Tiran was never be become as a well-mannered person.

Tiran was inquisitive to find that, whose plan was activated to trap him. Tiran had a reliable friend in the police station, and that barbarian police officer also had contributed the drug dealings of Tiran and had a beneficial profit. He found about the boyfriend of Tanya. Further he found that was a master plan of Tanya's boyfriend. Then Tiran had gone to Tanya's home, because Tiran's more stupid crimes and his stupid assistant's details had known by Tanya. Tiran had been taken more telephone calls over the official phone of his father's office. Tiran had discussed many crimes relative to drug dealing over that phone despite of Tanya was in front of the phone. Tiran had suspected that details would be pointed out of her boyfriend by Tanya. Then Tiran went to meet her without prior notice and he had threatened her, "If you will have revealed any kind of detail what you have early known about my businesses with your boyfriend, definitely you also will have to be faced the miserable destiny that happened to Nirasha." Tanya had known about Tiran's aspects, he would revenge as a cobra. Then Tanya didn't reveal any kind of secrets with anyone, because she bothered to protect her life and her family.

One day, Tiran was driving a cab on the highway, had impatiently tried to overtake another passenger bus on the way. The bus driver was in rather congestion and had to take about a few minutes to let the cab to overtake him. Then after overtaking the bus by Tiran had blocked the road and assaulted to the bus driver. Tiran was with liquor and harshly intoxicated. The innocent bus driver was hospitalized. There was a complaint to the police, but also no employed an action by the police. Once there was an accident with an innocent and poor motor cyclist by Tiran's cab, but also there wasn't taken a proper action by the police. At least they didn't allow to take a proper compensation for the damage of that bike. Once in a fuel queue, there was a severe lack of fuel and people had to stay on very long queue for long hours, probably days on the fuel queue. Tiran and a few of his friends had come with four vehicles and forcibly violated the rules and had taken full tanks of fuel. The innocent people had protested but the police had violently suppressed the people.

After about three years of Podde's death, about another victim death or disappearance had reported to the police. Sumith also had died or disappeared near by the bridge. According to gathered evidence, Sumith had gone a dropping hire with a person. While he is returning alone by his three-wheeler, He stopped a deserted place and lighted a cigarette. It has made mixed with ganja that means cannabis. Sumith usually addicted to cannabis. Cannabis, also known as marijuana is a psychoactive drug from taking the Cannabis plant. It's Native to Central and South Asia, and its plant has been used as a drug for intoxicate also can be helped to increase sexual emotions and delaying to the ejaculation when mixed them with tobacco and both recreational, entheogen purposes and in various traditional medicines for primeval times in the country. Cannabis can be used by smoking, vaporizing, within food. Having cannabis, there does not a bad smell like alcohol? But also had more unidentified feelings with over laughing. Then many drivers in the country usually had addicted to them. Because, the police didn't have a proper and advance measurement to catch them only reddish the eyes. Cannabis is mostly used recreationally or as a medicinal drug, although it may also be used for spiritual purposes. Physical effects include increased heart rate, difficulty breathing, nausea, and behavioral problems in children whose mothers' used cannabis during pregnancy. Short-term side effects may also include dry mouth and red eyes. Long-term adverse effects may include addiction, decreased mental ability. It is the most commonly used illegal drug in the world, though it is legal in some jurisdictions, with the highest use among adults.

Cannabis has various mental and physical effects, which include euphoria, altered states of mind and sense of time, difficulty concentrating, impaired short-term memory, impaired body movement and fine relaxation, and an increase in appetite. Onset of effects is felt within minutes when smoked, but may take up to 90 minutes when eaten. The effects last for two to six hours, depending on the amount used. At high doses, mental effects can include anxiety, delusions including ideas of reference, hallucinations, panic, paranoia, and psychosis. There is a strong relation between cannabis use and the risk of psychosis.

When he finished sucking the cigarette, He felt it very well. About nearly 5.00 pm, he started to return with a popular music of his radio. He wanted to have a cool drink because of the dry effect of cannabis, he stopped to take some snack in a small boutique and started to ride. He suddenly remembered the police regular check point which is established ahead. He should definitely omit it, because he had found some cannabis from his friend last day still in the cabin hall of the three-wheeler. Then he turned to the short cut which is laid on the ghostly bridge. When he was stopped by a beautiful girl who had worn a black scarf, worn with short skirt, thinner blouse and with a hand bag, he stopped and had captivated on her beautiful body and she also had worn rather a negligee. Sumith accepted the hire without any hesitation because he was an amatory man. The girl had requested to turn over to the deserted road where that perilous bridge was. Sumith didn't have showed any kind of suspected feelings or thoughts of the girl about the lustful emotions. He had fixed a secret mirror with his seat by focusing the hips and thighs of the passengers. That girl had worn a very short skirt and Sumith rode sweetly suffering them. He willingly waved the three-wheeler to be removed her thighs.

He rode along the way. He was requested by the girl to stop on the bridge and she said, "Let's stay here for a few minutes, I want to see the beauty of this area. Don't you like to feel the beauty of this environment?" Sumith said, "I like to see your beauty more than this environment, because you are very nice girl, tell me if you have a price". "I have an interesting price, I will tell you it soon", the girl said. Sumith filled with deep purpose to quench his lust by this girl who met him randomly. He looked her breasts with as like as a very greedy, lustful and as with a ravenous beast. The girl's white and round breasts invited to him. He saw then as blooming them for his lips. Her body tried to more and more motivate him because the breeze tried to open her buttons. The negligee skirt also obeyed to the compelling the breeze to open her thighs. They spoke a little time on the bridge about the attractions of surrounded area. "Where are you going in this moment, and is there your relations in this area", Sumith asked. "No! I don't have, but I like to conduct a new relationship with the boys like you, because the crocodiles that is under this bridge are very like to taste the boys like you!", She said. Then Sumith tried to hug and kiss her by saying, "Don't kidding me, I'll pay your price"! Suddenly, when on the bridge, she shouted, "Immoral dog! Can't you identify me! I am Nirasha! You betrayed me as a beast!" Sumith meticulously looked at her. Suddenly two strong cold hands squeezed his neck and pulled him down the bridge. The crocodiles cordially accepted him very happily and Sumith ever disappeared in a very short time among the brutal crocodiles. The next morning, the isolated three-wheeler near the bridge was found by the police on an information given by a nearby peasant.

The police investigations were launched. There wasn't any kind of evidence who or how to killed or whether disappeared or missing the body. As the other investigation files such as Nirasha, Kiththa and Podde, that file of Sumith also gathered in to the deep corner of the police cupboard as the unidentified homicidal cases with an unrevealed enigma. The police had found the mobile phone was being in the three-wheeler of Sumith, but also according to the call history of it, nothing had been found.

The election for electing the parliament members had arranged to be conducted by the government. Tiran's father also was nominated as a candidate by the governing party. The canvassing campaigns were being launched. The opposite candidate who was being helped by Nirasha's family had invited for a meeting in the village. Nirasha's father was the chief organizer of the meeting in the canvasing campaign. There was appeared the priority of votes may have been taken by the opposition candidate. Then Tiran's thuggery team had launched a collapsing campaign of the opposition's meetings. Then while conducting the meeting, Tiran's immoral team showed their vulgarity. Broke out the banners, threatened and assaulted the people and fired the stage. The meeting was postponed. The organizing committee had lodged a complaint to the police. But also, the police didn't have taken a proper action to be arrested them. Many meetings of the opposition had been faced such the miserable events, throughout the country, but the police were silent, even though they pretended the investigations are being conducted. The president and his foolish family also had secretly allowed to those violations. They had arranged to provide a quarter of bottle of arrack, a rice packet with some money for the voters to be increased their votes. These illegitimate family had been done these enticements to be cheated the innocent people. Some stupid people had betrayed and slaved their dignity such on the tricks. Having with the agitations, riots, quarrels and with highly violations of voting rules that the election was conducted.

Eventually, the opposition was able to win the election. Tiran's father and his immoral period was sunk in the deepest sea. The winners were imagined, there will be approached a chiliastic era of this country.
According to the regulations of newly parliament, the corrupted officials who had committed with unjustifiable, heinous acts and loyal duties of the departments, were transferred or demoted. The current governor was a very justifiable, law abiding and strict person. He had a real enthusiasm to be developed the country by repelling the misconducted officials. He doesn't genuflect with the overseas, when getting the decisions to be up-lifted the country. The officials who had appointed by the political purposes of the former government without adequate educating qualifications were kept their suitable places. There were 182 police officials in the police department who appointed illegally or non-educated and non-qualified by the former government.

The police Inspector, **Palitha Iddagoda** also had taken a promotion and had been made an appointment to the police station of Nirasha's area. Because the former I.P was demoted and transferred to remote area on was being disqualified for the post. He was the most corrupted officer who was there among that politicalized immoral officials. According to his historical reports, he had mostly earned by helping and contributing with drug dealers. Iddagoda was a talented, prestigious and well-educated person with adequate qualifications.

When I have received the message of his appointment, I intended to take his support for revealing the Nirasha's case. Then I decided to have taken a call to him at a suitable time. Palitha Iddagoda was an honest, well-principled officer. He never had allowed his officials to take bribes from innocent people. Because as I know, I early had taught him in my dramatical lessons when he involved with my stage drama, how should a person dedicate his power for the deployment of the own country. Because the theme of my drama was directly aimed to criticized the immoral, stupid and corrupted officials and politicians. He acted with a main character of that drama based on a brave, nun-flexible, principled, and honest military officer. I remember, when a rehearsal, once he said and appreciate of that character, because he expected to involve with the forces of the country. Whenever, he had determined to whenever be an officer followed the same character. He strictly had ordered to arrange the immediate besieging events of the details of drug dealers.
I took a call to I.P Iddagoda and got an appointment to meet him. I went to the relevant police station with my Principal, Mr. Dinuja and Prishan. Because I wanted to introduce him to Iddagoda and discuss about Nirasha's hidden disappearing suit. Then we were able describe to Iddagoda about all heinous acts of Tiran and I

requested him to pay his attention about the case. I didn't request it as an official level but also as a close friend. Then he amicably agreed to involve into the case and find the details about it. Then, Iddagoda suggested to Prishan be made an urgent entry with the police records about Nirasha's case. He further explained, you shouldn't feel any hesitation to make a complaint due to the former every loyal officials of the felonies had almost transferred away from the police station. Prishan was committed to lodge a complaint against to Tiran. There wasn't any allegedly direct complaint before against to Tiran according to the police records. After that complaining, Iddagada promised us, that all the illicit undisclosed events of Tiran and his father will be investigated at the near future. He promised also to appoint a few officials of the police to spying whereabouts of Tiran. But also, according to that complaint of Prishan, Tiran won't be arrested by the police without the authenticable evidence. Iddagoda wanted to arrest the felonies with unbreakable evidence because Tiran and his father were the former influential people in the area. Before concluding the discussion, Iddagoda ordered an officer to find Nirasha's File. Then we left the police station. We had to drop Prishan into his home. While we were returning to Prishan's home by the car of Dinija, we discussed meet again to continue and chase the complaint about Tiran.

We dropped him into his home and withdrawn soon because we had the appointed classes in the evening.

Tiran and his friends had to restrict their illegal businesses. I.P Iddagoda had led a few officers to spy on Tiran. They were able to collect more information about Tiran's drug dealings within a few months.

Tiran was a moderator for drugs. He had a modified farm house in his farm. Twice a month usually, a small lorry had been transported fertilizer and animal forage in to the farm. The police had strategically employed a spying labor into the farm as an employee. The spying unit had collected the suspicious lorry by his details. One evening, the lorry came to the farm and started to unload. The police team that early managed to raid the place and ambushed for the mission. While unloading the lorry, the police team nabbed the illicit bundle of liquor bottles and bags with cannabis. Cannabis is an illegal and alleged to be possessed according to the country law suit. The lorry with the illicit stuff and the employees were arrested soon. The owner of the farm, Tiran was disappeared. He absconded the police for a long time.

The farm land that was committed to the illegal matter doesn't have a legalized land deed. It was possessed to the government. Tiran's father had made an illegal deed for it. Typically, the influential politicians and the government officials are being involved to do such this shameless work in this country. Then he also had to be arrested by the police. When Tiran also willingly appeared to the police and both of them were to present to the court. They were released on a huge bail under many conditions as their lawyer's request. The future trial dates had been given by the court. However, they will be definitely released from the trial because the police will be unable to find the real evidence to prove the offence. If the police will be able to reveal the adequate details, the found details will not be submitted as the evidence in to the court because they also would be suppressed by the thieves.

A former president and his relatives of this country also had involved such the illegal matters, but also the current president had said that, there aren't any evidence against of them to prove these thefts.
I.P Iddagoda tried to find evidence for Nirasha"s case. Although, the details were deleted or the important pages of the file had been disappeared. Otherwise, all the suspicions had died such as Kiththa, Podde and Sumith. Tiran was the only person who remains in living, and the body of Nirasha was not still found. Anyone doesn't know what had happened her.
During this period, in a one morning, a farmer who has typically involved with fishing that perilous river bank where the haunting bridge of Nirasha, had seen a part of torn ladies hand bag in the mud. He had taken it and clealy washed. He was able to find the damaged identity card of Nirasha in it. He had submitted it to the police. Then I.P iddagoda had activated soon and sent a few prepared officials to find more details. The officials had to find more evidence in a very dangerous condition as the thicker crocodile attacks were reported from the river. They laboriously checked the riverbank, could find a dressing part of Nirasha. Having identified them by her parents, Nirasha's case was aroused again.

Time had been flown quickly. The complaint that was lodged by Prishan against to Tiran was renewed but the police couldn't find more evidence abuot her body. The complaint sunk in the same cupboard, because there weren't any kind of authenticable evidence against to Tiran. I.P Iddagoda also was being made his regret, because he doesn't leave the case willingly. I also couldn't involve for the case due to my son was preparing for hid advance level examination. My daughter was able to take an appointment as an English teacher in an international English medium school that was being conducted in this country. Then I had to provide her to transport facilities. Meanwhile there had been started to outbreak the Covid 19 throughout the world. All of the schools of the country had to immediately close temporary. The governmental officials, school teachers and film halls including theaters had to close. The tuition institutes, wedding ceremonials and all of the projects those gathering people had to restrict. Unfortunately, I also became a huge critical event due to emerge a poor economic condition. But, before long, I was able to reproduce my economy by using the internet media to be conducted the classes. We had to restrict at least two years of time duration due to that pandemic. The infected many people had to die at the initially. The imported vaccines had been given to the people by the government. There has been reported that, a huge amount of money had been misused by the former governors while importing them. We can have an opinion about how such beasts had governed our country at that period. The mendacious governors had stopped every essential importing things by telling lies to the people as they are going to create a non-poisoned country at being stopped the inorganic fertilizer import. However, the country has been become into a bankrupt position at this moment. The seven thunder lightening will be applied them and they will be welcomed by the hell as soon possible. Some officials of the airport had taken the bribes to immigrate the infected people into the country without being conducted the tests for Covid. These corrupted all governmental officials and the politicians will be able to hold their last banquet at the Hell Gate. If the God or religion is true, I wish to send them into the hell.

Tiran and his father had temporary silent mood, because the political power had lost of their party. Some of thieves of the people's taxes had stealthily left the country. The responsible officials of the government had allowed them to leave the country on money.

Some governmental teachers of the country had started to emit their economic pressure on the students by unjustifiably punishing them and recklessly teaching. Some students were punished considered them as beasts by the teachers. When reading the investigation reports, such the immoral teachers had been played the key roles of executioners. One day, my son went to school in the morning. He called me about 10.00 am, because he was drastically punished with a rattan by the disciplinary in-charge of the school. The punished rattan marks had on his hands. I went to the school at the moment. While I was going there, that the disciplinary in-charge suddenly started to scold me and he threatened me, "Go to anyway and take any legal action, I punished your son because he had bring a mobile phone into the school premises instead it was banned by the government. I have activated on the government circulars that previously issued by the education department." I wanted to explain with him why I have sent such a small button phone with him to the school. But he didn't try to listen me and ululated as a mad fox. I went to the principal's office and explained why I have sent a phone with my son. There was a Chess tournament in a remote school where established far away from the city. My son and other some students had been prepared to delegate that event for his school. The previous day I went to the school and I met the teacher who works as the Chess games in-charge. I asked her, whether a teacher will be participated tomorrow for the event to fetch the students as the guidance of the students. She said, "Definitely, nothing!" I asked, "Would you have arrange the transport facilities by the school bus that we have early provided it to the school by the funds of school developing society?" She said, "Definitely nothing." Then I noted it and thought, how the students could return their homes after the tournament, as it will be conducting until the evening. Otherwise, the tournament will be held very far away from the own school. I also had more appointed classes in the evening. I supposed to take my son after the tournament. But, the problem was, how I can take the information about the time or from where we can meet after the event. Then I decided to send a small phone with my son. But also all those arrangements should have been done by the teacher in-charge of the event. How could they omit their responsibility without even a participation of any each teachers? I sent the relevant phone with my son to be solved all the issues. I have given the necessary instruction to my son, when you enter the class, hand over the phone to the class teacher and take it when you leave the school for that event. Unexpectedly, there was an assembly before start the school in the morning. Then, my son had leave his bag with the phone in his classroom and had run to the assembly as the delaying also might be a punishable reason by that immoral disciplinary in-charge. The assembly had been arranged in the school ground. My son had participated the assembly, therefore he didn't have met the class teacher at the time. While the assembly was performing, the prefects had checked the bags in the class room and had found the phone. The disciplinary in-charge didn't allow me or my son, why he had taken a phone into the class. He threatened me as a dictator, and he activated as if the school premises is his own property. He shouted me, "Go and complain to anyone, I have properly followed the circulars, then I don't fear for them." I went to meet the principal and complained about it. He also didn't accept the failure of his staff. Then I came to home and started to find the said circulars from the internet. I couldn't find a circular with any kind of regulations about the phone usage of students in a school. But also, there was a circular about punishing the students. According to them, on any reason, the teachers didn't have a right to bodily, which means corporal punishing to the students. I further checked that rule of In loco parentis. I had more anger because the disciplinary in-charge had asked about my career position before punishing my son, and had scolded him, "The tutors are going to make the country, if you can tell him to complain anyone against me." While punishing the son, "I am the OIC of the disciplinary section of this school, your father is a private tutor. What can he do?" He had insult me. I wanted to tell him, my students had received more successful results in the exams. Otherwise his own kids also were attending the tuition classes. If the school teachers cover the subjects properly, with well-made tutorials, why our students involving for the tuition classes even missing the school times? Then I wrote an impulsive letter to the principal, and with a copy was sent to that immoral disciplinary OIC by referring the said circulars. However, the phone which I have sent was detained by that OIC. It was not a stolen good. It has received me as a present of a parent of his son's previous achievement with my guidance. Then can he detain the phone with him? Then I finally suggest them, whenever the student will be leaving the school, that detained phone should return to the student and it will be more ethical.

There is a combination between the age of the child on the one side and the teacher's responsibility and liability for it on the other side. In that event, the principal had missed his responsibility about the protection of the students who had prepared to participation for the Chess tournament in a remote school on the students protection and guidance. The chess teacher also had omit her due responsibility. The disciplinary OIC also should have been an inquisitive person to the event, why this student had brought a phone into the school. But, without being inquiring any kind of the based details or students' explanation of the background, why has he drastically punished my son? The young student must obey the teacher, and the teacher may use the proper strategies expected and tolerated in the community to manage the child's behavior. The child's physical safety is entrusted to the school and to the teacher, who thus become legally liable for the safety of the child, as far as negligence can be proved against them.

In the event of corporal or physically harming punishment, is a local and inappropriate attitude and it has established among the frustrated and tired teachers a wide range of expected and permissible inherent aspect on the part of the teacher. In most countries of the world, young children may be punished by a limited application of physical pain at or on their buttocks or palms by the teacher or school principal applying a wooden ruler. I never allow to punish the students by using a rattan, wooden ruler, or whip of one kind or another way. But there are some systems that explicitly bar a teacher from using corporal punishment. This seems most common in large cities; the teacher in a rural or small-city school is more suitable to be expected to use physical measures for managing pupil behavior. As students become older, their behavior is not suitable to be managed by physical measures, and they are more likely to receive detention or be suspended from classes or expelled from school. This is the common last resort in the upper years of the secondary school and in the reputable universities.

Meanwhile, Prishan called me and gave me a fabulous information. According to his description, I wanted to authenticate the information. After I took a call to I.P Iddagoda and known more details about the event. He told me to have that morning newspaper for more information. I suddenly get brought the newspaper and started to read it.

There was a wedding ceremony in a reputed hotel. Many prestigious politicians, rich businessmen, and other reputable people had participated in it. The bridegroom had worn a European dress. The bride was a beautiful, nice young girl who was the youngest daughter of a rich businessman in the country. The traditional ceremonial customs had been arranged at 10.00 am. Having concluded the ceremonial customs, there was a symposium for the invitees with delicious banquet. The couple and the relatives enjoyed the ceremony because they had arranged a huge musical event to singing and dancing who have encourage to enjoy. After that symposium, the new couple had planned to make their honeymoon at a large hotel nearby a large reservoir. Because they wanted to stay freely for three days in that attractive place. Having being concluded the ceremony, the couple had reached the hotel around 6.30 p.m. Some of a few reliable friends of the bridegroom were invited by the bridegroom for chatting with them. The addiction to alcohol has emerged with the bridegroom. The friends had started the usual behavior with liquor. After the dinner, within approximately two hours, the friends had left the hotel. The couple was more tired and tedious, because the ceremonial events at the day time. Then they went to the bed as soon as possible. The next day they enjoyed their honeymoon freely. In the evening they used the swimming pool to enjoy. Tiran usually spent his time with his wife but with always intoxicated. He had addicted to that immoral and stupid life. His wife ignored his behavior. Tiran had invited a few friends at the evening party. The party has successfully conducted.

The next morning, that fabulous event had revealed. I had an arrangement to visit our tuition institute in the evening as I appointed an additional class for past paper discussion. Having concluded it, I went to Prishan's home with Dinuja, because we wanted to know further about the event.

I had collected the newspaper with me. There was an outburst incident which promulgated on the media and in newspaper, "The mysterious death of provincial councilor's son." Actually, I didn't have ever believed that the event of campaigning posters of our institute, and encountering Nirasha with me, will be a part of such a serious secret.

Prishan continued, "Here are the other paper articles about the death of Tiran". He showed a few articles, and said, "These papers had been collected by my mother".

"Okay! What had happened to Tiran?" I asked finally. The newspapers didn't have revealed more information about the case, because of the police investigations still were being conducted. Then we wanted to be found more information about the incident. Dinuja decided to stay in that hotel for two days. Then I got a suitable night dress from Prishan. While we are travelling, we went to Dinuja's home and we collected the other needed stuff. We went to that hotel where the wedding ceremony was conducted. But we didn't reveal the reason with the staff of the hotel why we attended or about we are scanning the event. We reserved a room for two days and boarded in the room. I took a call to my wife and informed her about my absent of home. We planned to make friendships with the manager and other relevant staff. Specially, with the bell-boy of that wedding couple. We were able to gather significant details from the hotel. The relevant bell-boy's exposure was made us into an unbelievable position. We had to spent some money to be tamed the bell-boy to get the relevant details.

The bride was a charm and innocent girl. No more haste, kindly faced to the prevailing events. While Tiran and his friends were in the living room of the hotel with enjoying, Tiran's warm bride had entered their separated room for a little rest with a washing herself. She was tired and felt sleepy because of the day time enjoyments. They had involved a few times personal enjoyments with their marriage. Then she wanted to get rest.

Having concluded the friends' party, Tiran came to the bedroom. Tiran also had felt just tired and sleepy. Tiran gave her some liquor, to drink if she was tired. She willingly drank it slowly.

Tiran tried to kiss her. "Let's sleep now, I am not in my mood! We will enjoy every missing things tomorrow, please! I am feeling like someone is trying to invade me, I can see a very beautiful girl is in front of me. Let me please allow to sleep now!" his wife requested. They had gone to bedroom at about 11.30 p.m. Tiran's wife felt a strange mood of her mind. She was ascended by Nirasha. Then she was extremely changed with her behavior. She talked to Tiran in a very loving manner. Tiran got up suddenly, and saw his wife as if really Nirasha. She told him, I like to walk in the moonbeams, let's go out and enjoy. She compelled to Tiran in a very lovely and sexy manner. Tiran also agreed with her and got ready to go out. The bell-boy said with us, that girl who was leaving with Tiran at the night is not appeared as the girl who appeared at the daytime as Tiran"s bride. Because she didn't directly see anyone or anything, worked a strange style and had a very proud appearance. Tiran behaved like a loony man and looked like they wanted to escape from the hotel. The hotel servants were surprised, because why this new couple wanted to go out in this moment. But finally they had decided, if that is their pleasure. Then the new couple had left from the hotel at about 2.00 am.

In the morning, Tiran's wife felt a hard cold. She felt a terrible condition. She was not in a luxurious room when they getting bed. She felt a very dangerous emotion. She slightly saw, she was in a car. She felt a severe thirsty and looked for water but nothing. There was a half left bottle of liquor, she drank it without considering the bitterness. She couldn't get to presence of her mind. Suddenly she identified, she was in a car and the driver's door was being opened. But also, the driver didn't on the seat, then she opened her side door and looked here and there. The moon was very attractively being shined in the sky, a very cold breeze came to the car. She thought, Tiran may be nearby the car and he wanted to surprise her at this moment. She could see the sandals that was using by Tiran at the night, was there in the car. She heard a flowing sound of stream and some struggling sounds of fishes in the water. She looked the floor soon. She frightened a lot because the car was on a relatively narrow bridge. She suddenly felt a hard drowsiness. She closed the opened doors of the car on that sleepy. She thought this may be a dreadful nightmare and turned to sleep again.

Unexpectedly, she woke up from sleeping within half an hour again on mosquitos' stinging. She thought a moment, looked surrounded area only the view from the car window. That also was a nighttime with a shining full moon. What is this place? She was very scared and impressed. She had yelled as well as she could, she couldn't have understood, where was Tiran and what had happened to him? The helpless and innocent girl had frightened and completely confused. She thought she was dreaming the most dangerous nightmare that she had ever seen. She had victimized with stinging the mosquitoes. She remembered that she closed the door as the opposite door had opened. She felt this moment, actually that was not a dream. But she was thoughtful to be closed the previously opened shutters of the car soon. She thought by conjecture, that Tiran will be back into the car soon. She again lost her consciousness.
As usual, the sun had gradually arisen by defeating the darkness of the dawn. While maturing the sun, a motorcyclist came across this narrow bridge, unexpectedly

there was a car on the bridge. He examined the car; he saw a young girl was sleeping in the car. He meticulously observed the car and around. He was a familiar person into this area. He saw an inundated body of a man laid under the bridge. He didn't try to touch anything, because he had known past events about this bridge. The man had a mobile phone. He took a call to the police soon because he was unable to cross the stream as the car had blocked the road. Before arriving at the police, many people came to see the event. They were able to examine, that the young woman in the car was alive.

A servant that means bell-boy who served the wedding couple the last night had given a statement to the police about a strange behavior that appeared from Tiran and the bride last night. He had left the hotel with his wife, murmuring, "I am so sorry Nirasha, I am coming with you. Please don't leave me here alone, let's go soon, I would like to walk with you as far as we can". The servant had guessed and thought that strange behavior was his usual routine. The security guard said that the gate had to open according to the passers' request. Otherwise, there was a girl in the car like a beauty queen. Then, the guard had not gone to inquire about their leaving. The gate keeper had decided, they may be leaving for their early appointed necessity. Otherwise interrupting or preventing the guests is not allowed them by the management.

According to the information received over the phone, the police found that the inundated corpse of Tiran was there under that small bridge where I had enjoyed the environment at least 8 years ago. The police investigations had been started. The girl had hospitalized by the police with her parental guidance. The police investigations were being continued.

Mobile phones had been used during that time by the people. The rich people used to buy smart mobile phones. The other civilians had used to the button mobile phones. Tiran and his wife generally used smart mobile phones.

Tiran was driving the car. His wife, Ruchirani was sitting in the front passenger seat. Ruchirani was an innocent girl, growing up with her parental guidance. She didn't have an educated background that much. She was an extreme and timid girl without self-esteem or self-confidence. Having being loosed concentration and with Ruchirani's childish mind, Definitely, Nirasha's spirit might have already easily ascended to Ruchirani's soul. Therefore, Tiran began to see her as Nirasha. Her voice also may have been converted to voice like Nirasha. Now, gradually, Tiran was completely dominated by Nirasha. Nirasha had improved her concentration by meditating while she was studying in the university.

She had highly improved the knowledge about mesmerism. She had composed an article about hypnotherapy. Because of that, she had followed a deep philosophy of a very unique religious leader. As I think, that was the reason, she was able to appear in front of the people as a living being from time to time. She had a levitating power entering and invading into another person's mind.

I wanted to study about mesmerism. The curiosity to explore about something, and that curiosity will be arisen me to enthusiasm for committed me to find it.

The manner or power of gaining control in capturing someone's subliminal that means subconscious mind or his presence mentality over someone's personality, mind behavior or actions, as in hypnosis or suggestion can be defined as mesmerism. The action or process of inducting someone to a position of a state of consciousness in which a person apparently losses the own power of voluntary action and is highly responsive to suggestion. Its use in therapy to recover suppressed memories to allow charming of behavior by suggestion. The mesmerism is a reputable science to be cured many mental depressions. But also, this science should use very carefully, because the person who was mesmerized, getting a temporary sleeping with his presence mind and surfing his own previous souls. It may a very dangerous, event because they have to take a service of hypnotist to return into presence mind.

While they were traveling with arguing along the way, Nirasha was narrating, "I didn't have a purpose to be killing your friends, Podde, and kiththa, then I only wanted to reveal the violent murder you did to me, but when I appeared to them, they were very seriously frightened to me. They were mentally fallen down with their fear. Because of that excessive fear, they would have approached to quickly shock and died with highly increased blood pressure with heart attacks. Otherwise, I didn't ever appear them on the bridge. I let them go a little ahead". Tiran couldn't understand about how the mood of Ruchirani change to Nirasha's shape. Because he also converted in a loss thoughtful mind with Nirasha's mighty.

There was a call to Tiran. "Hello", Tiran replied. "Don't, please.... Please don't disturb me. I am with my Nirasha! I want to go and speak with her. I will call you later." The friend who had taken a call at the time wanted to make a hoax about the new couple. Although, he didn't really have known the name of Nirasha or Ruchirani. Because the caller was only a friend of Tiran. Tiran had brought a remains bottle, and he took little by little. By this time the car was reaching the narrow bridge. Tiran's intoxication had been highly increased. Really on the bridge, his mind recognized the reality. "Even now, I don't need revenge from you, if you would accept the offense in the court." "Oh! Here is Nirasha! But we killed you, on this bridge and pulled you to the water! No, really must be you are her ghost." He was heavily and terribly frightened. His heart was highly flamed. He wanted to escape from her. He opened the door. He didn't see anything that was there out of the car. He Jumped!! He had jumped directly on to the river because the car had stopped on the verge of the bridge. The highly intoxication of Tiran didn't allow to made restore his presence, he didn't have tried to survive because his severe unconsciousness with cannabis and with liquor. He had been charged on anesthesia and sunk in the deep water.

Finally we decided, Nirasha's inhuman soul would have been reached her freely emancipation by achieving her expectation to be punished the heinous felonies of an innocent girl.

Tanya had the information about the death of Tiran. She suddenly decided to reveal all the hidden details of Tiran, because the early life threaten by Tiran to Tanya's family had ridded with Tiran's death. She told the all details with her boyfriend without being any kind of hesitation. Then, Tanya had to provide a statement to the police as the request of her boyfriend and with the inspection of I.P Iddagoda. A written copy of Tanya's statement was attached with Nirasha's homicidal file in the deep corner of that police cupboard because it was the one and only verbal evidence had revealed by Tiran about Nirasha's murder. "However, if that statement of Tanya would have been early submitted to us, Tiran would have been caught to the police", I.P Iddagoda said.

Curiosity is my weapon. Especially about exploring the ghosts, apparitions, and inhuman souls. Then, that night I hardly spent in Dinuja's home. Extremely I wanted to research the relevant place. I profoundly decided to cross that difficult road bypassing the main road. In the morning, at about 10.30, I came onto the above-mentioned bridge. I childishly expected Nirasha again on the bridge. But she will never come again because she had already revealed the "murderers of Nirasha". Can you understand, why did she appear to me that night? She wanted to give a clue to Prishan's family, "Her soul was being striven to reveal the murderers"!

I again wanted to see Nirasha's photograph, because I drastically wanted to memorize that the girl who appeared in front of me was really was she. Then I requested to prishan, "Please show me a photo that most closely taken with her. He gave me one of them, had taken early three days before her death at the university. "Yes, indeed. I couldn't believe my eyes. When I leave her alone on the bridge, she was looking at me innocently, like this." Here is, **"Nirasha, The ghost of the bridge!"**

Then I took my phone camera and saved her picture in my gallery. Although it would be deleted whenever on the memory chip of my phone. She will never delete from my memory.

I will be back with my next books, **"The Flamed agreement with a Blacksmith."**

And, **"The Enegma of Planet Septica."**

I wish you will be interested in those stories too.

- **Written By Mahesh Munasinghe.**
- **Edited By Bawnatha Munasinghe.**

www.ingramcontent.com/pod-product-compliance
Lightning Source LLC
LaVergne TN
LVHW041231150826
845673LV00008B/2358
* 9 7 9 8 8 4 2 1 6 2 1 4 7 *